And

Love

Triangle
Continues

Dr. Vishwa Prakash

PARTRIDGE
A Penguin Company

Partridge books may be ordered through booksellers or by contacting:

Partridge India
Penguin Books India Pvt. Ltd
11, Community Centre, Panchsheel Park, New Delhi 110017
India
www. partridgepublishing. com
Phone: 000.800.10062.62

Chapter 1

'Pradeep,' Vibha pushed open the door greeted him smile spread over her sensuous lips and before Pradeep could yell a word she entered the room. Pradeep glanced over her and said smiling, 'Good morning, how are you?'

'I am fine Pradeep,' said Vibha coming closer to the table where Pradeep was reading a book. 'What are you reading?' She asked, and without waiting for the answer she bent her head forward looking at the open book trying to figure out the contents. 'So are you performing any new operation?' She asked pulling the vacant chair out a bit and sat over that, smiling sensuously.

'Yes,' Pradeep answered with arrogance biting his lower lip, 'Triple Flap Vaginoplasty. You would be pleased to know that he had been invited to deliver a lecture in Sholapur subject being Triple Flap Vaginoplasty.'

'Sholapur! In which part of country it is situated?' She enquired.

'It is situated in Maharashtra,' Pradeep told.

'Oh! And you are going alone over there?' She asked shaking her head a bit so that hair came in front of his cheeks.

'You may come along with me,' Pradeep said put a book mark on the page and closed the book. It was actually Journal of Obstetrics and Gynaecology Research in which his research paper was published. Pradeep was a plastic surgeon with special interest in female genital reconstruction and had developed many newer techniques in the field.

His interest in the field started when he was doing his internship after passing MBBS in the medical college where he came across many patients who had undergone tubal ligations and developed different types of the problems after the procedure, few developed menstrual pain and others were having pain off and on in the abdomen. The senior gynaecologists rebuked at them alleging that they had become mental patients after tubal ligations. Pradeep were not convinced. All the women could not have become psychiatric, the Gynaecologists should take over the issue and try to find out a cause.

'Pradeep, where are you lost?' Vibha interrupted his thought process.

He smiled but grimly this time. 'Vibha, I am amazed that no doctor ever thought of developing and working to reconstruct female genitals . . . No body! Why?'

'It was left for you,' she said and giggled.

'I agree with you God has left it for me to reconstruct, and then changing the topic he asked, 'Vibha will you like to have tea or coffee?'

She smiled, pursed her lips and said, 'Tea would do.'

Pradeep pressed the bell to call Pappu.

Pappu . . . Pappu was entrusted with the work of serving tea to all the consultants of the department of Plastic Surgery. He was not hospital employee but worked in the department whole day, supplying tea and some eatables to the consultants and resident doctors. Pappu entered, 'What should I bring sir?'

'Pappu bring two very tasty teas.'

'OK sir,' said he glancing at Vibha. He knew she did not belong to the department of Plastic Surgery but hovered around Pradeep very frequently, they were no husband and wife even then she was always seen in his chamber, he thought but did not say a word to anybody. Pradeep was a senior doctor any wrong statement about him might cause problems to him.

'Pradeep you created a new subspecialty and snatched it from Gynaecologists,' said Vibha and changed her posture in the chair.

'I am not in agreement with you I have not snatched it from Gynaecologists rather shown them the way to treat the incurable conditions of female genitals, many of the procedures could be learnt by them, others could be done by us; aim being to give the best results rather than confusing the patients.'

'I agree to you,' Vibha agreed.

Pappu entered holding two cups of tea kept one cup in front of Vibha and another in front of Pradeep.

'Any other eatables to be brought sir?' He asked politely.

'No,' said Pradeep taking sip from cup.

Pradeep lifted his hand to give one cup to Vibha, when she was clutching the cup his fingers touched hers and he intertwined the fingers; the innumerable waves were flowing inside him, and he felt throbbing pulsations, she also felt same throbbing in her feminine ecstatic valley; he kept on holding her fingers and caressed.

After some time Vibha cautioned, 'Tea would fall over us.'

Pradeep came to life and released her fingers. Vibha lifted the cup to take to her mouth and took a sip. Pradeep got to his toes to go on the back of Vibha and put his hand over her cheek, slowly caressing down over her inviting and luscious lips.

Pradeep, Ah! She wanted to say, but the words were cut by teeth. She was in mirth, caressing by man, her man, her heart throb, were sending innumerable waves inside her putting her to embers. She pushed her neck backwards. Pradeep slid his fingers over her neck and got chance to insinuate beneath the white protective wrap over her bosom, when she caught holds his hand, and looked up grinning . . .

Pradeep strolled back to his chair and lifted the cup to take other sip.

'What are you doing tonight?' Vibha asked.

Pradeep looked straight in her eyes, 'For what reason you are enquiring?'

'If you are not busy in some other work come for dinner at my apartment.'

Pradeep frowned, 'for dinner? At present I don't remember any work which I have to do in the evening, but why are you inviting for dinner, to celebrate some special occasion?'

'Every day is special occasion, come for the dinner tonight.'

He twitched his lips and nodded in affirmation.

After finishing tea she put the cup on the table and got to her toes, 'My boss will eat me if I am late, so I should hurry up.'

'You should not worry so much for her.'

She grinned and turned to go out of his chamber and walked to her department.

She was lecturer in department of Gynaecology and Pradeep was lecturer in department of Plastic Surgery, both were class fellows since first year MBBS. Vibha was his table partner in first year of MBBS and since then she was in love with him. Pradeep did not like her initially, but afterward developed soft corner for her. However that soft corner never meant that he would marry to her.

Vibha on the other hand was bent upon marrying Pradeep, if she married, she would marry to Pradeep and nobody else, and if he did not marry she would better remain celibate for whole of her life.

Registrar knocked at the door of chamber. Pradeep called him in. 'Sir Will you take round of the patients now or afterward?' Registrar asked.

'I think I should take the round now, he said and got to his toes, lifting the white apron came out of the chamber with registrar.

'How are the patients?' He asked on the way to the ward.

'All the patients are alright. For operation tomorrow; there is one patient of vaginoplasty.'

'Vaginoplasty! I mean the patient who has come from Delhi?' He asked.

'Yes sir.' Registrar agreed.

'Ok vaginoplasty patient is one of the patients for operation, what about other patients for operation?' Pradeep asked.

"Sir there is another patient for breast reconstruction, should we post her for surgery tomorrow?'

Walking through the long corridor they came to the ward, the plastic surgery ward was having six cubicles, and one of the cubicle was allotted to Pradeep to admit his patients; every cubicle was having six beds.

Sister came for taking the orders, first patient was suffering with vaginal agenesis, the same patient which registrar had told to Pradeep, for vaginoplasty. 'I will do Triple Flap Vaginoplasty,' Pradeep told.

Next patient was suffering from cervical incompetence and as a result was having recurrent abortions . . . Pradeep had planned cervicorrhaphy. 'Sir, should I post this patient for tomorrow?' Asked registrar. 'No,' Pradeep told him not to post the patient for operation next day as he was in mood to operate the patient on some other day. Next patient was for abdominoplasty she was having bad hernia of the abdomen and was referred from Gynae department for hernia correction along with abdominoplasty.

After checking up all patients Pradeep came back to his chamber, where he found an envelope pushed in his chamber from the chink in the door. He lifted the envelop from the floor and brought out the papers from inside the envelop. It was brochure of Fem Gen Con (Female genital conference) which was scheduled to be held at Pune, he went through the contents and decided to present the research paper on Triple Flap Vaginoplasty. He would ask Vibha to present something or else he would make her co-author of his paper so that she got the permission to attend the conference.

And she could stay with him in the same room, he grinned; the dalliance activity crept in his brain. She had never permitted him to explore her feminine body beyond a certain limit; this time if she stayed with him in Pune would she allow him to find out details of anatomy of her body she should . . .

Vibha came to the chamber after taking the clinical round (To check on the patients admitted in the ward) of her patients with her senior. 'Oh! You are back,' Pradeep commented plainly.

'Yes, why? Why are you aghast at finding me over here?' She commented sarcastically.

'I am not aghast,' Pradeep yelled 'I was thinking that we might go together to fem Gen Con conference.'

Vibha pulled out the chair and sat over that. Pradeep cast a glance at her breasts, he had not paid any attention to her in morning; finding him ogling at her she blushed.

'Hey what are you ogling at? Behave as a nice child,' Vibha retorted.

'I am a nice child want to suck . . . ,' Pradeep answered but cut the sentence in half and decided not to spell other half of the sentence.

'Suck! Suck what?' Vibha cut her lower lip with teeth and snorted.

'Milk,' he said hurriedly.

'Pradeep,' she rebuked at him, 'You have seen my pointed heel sandals, and I will slap you with these over your head.

'Vibha there is brochure of conference FemGenCon, which is being held in Pune this time,' Pradeep changed the topic of discussion. 'Will you like to attend it? I think you should attend it.'

Vibha was noncommittal.

'What happened? Why no response from you.'

'I will decide in a day or two, how could I take the decision immediately. 'Then she said, 'I am going back to my apartment, and will wait for you at dinner, 'she informed and rose to her feet to come out of the chamber.

Pradeep, the most eligible bachelor of the hospital, was her heart throb since first year of MBBS when she met him for the first time, she was infatuated with him, and by chance they both were allotted the same dissection table in the Anatomy department. 'You are from which city?' she had asked to which he had not answered, pretending not being able to listen. 'Pradeep,' she had asked little loudly, 'You belong to which place?'

Pradeep looked at her and was not much impressed, did not answer. Vibha kept mum, alright he was not interested to answer, one day he would answer, answer everything what she would have asked . . . and she giggled in herself.

And years have passed. He had become plastic surgeon working as lecturer in plastic surgery department, yet he was not answering many a times, though she was firm that she would make him to answer all her questions one day, she was also stubborn. Walking on the road she took turn to left to reach her apartment. Fishing out the key from bag she unlocked the door and entered inside and bolted the door on her back. One day she would force him to answer every question which she would ask, she giggled . . . Let her see who won at last . . . her love or his neglect for love. What she would cook for dinner that day, she opened the fridge and cast a glance to find out the eatables stored in there, potatoes and tomatoes were in plenty, milk, what about milk, she peeped into one of the cupboard, it was not there. She should cook the kheer first and rest of the preparations could be made in the evening. She should arrange for the milk.

While the kheer was being cooked she sauntered to the bathroom and removed all her clothes to take a nice wash. She saw her naked body through the mirror and flushed cupped her breasts and slowly caressed them to reach at nipples and put them between thumb and fingers to caress, as if they were being caressed by Pradeep not by her . . . . Ah she was in mirth, why he was not indulging in dalliance. Hey but not before marriage, she was strict. He had to marry to her first, if he wanted to indulge in dalliance activity with her. She opened the tap and filled the bucket with water and took out the water in the mug to splash all-over her body. Pradeep why did you not come, come and caress me, my body, my breasts, my thighs and my feminine beauty, deep inside; come Pradeep she was dying to feel him and his masculine hard organ, Vibha was thinking.

In the evening Pradeep walked over to apartment of Vibha glanced all-around on the way to find if anybody was there to find him entering Vibha's apartment. As there was nobody around, Pradeep walked hurriedly and mountained the flight of stairs, came in front of her apartment, pressed the call bell and waited for her to open the door. Vibha opened the door and made the way for him to enter inside and closed the door after him. 'Come have a seat,' she offered the seat; he walked over to sit over sofa, which wavered with the weight of Pradeep. 'What would you like to take, I mean hot or cold?' Vibha asked 'Why you are so formal Vibha, come and sit with me, talk to me,' Pradeep requested to her to sit with him.

Vibha sat in front of him, 'I also wanted to talk, but you never make space to me,' she was thinking in the heart . . . yes, today he may talk about marriage, our marriage for which she was longing for long 'Yes, let us talk,' said Vibha.

'Arre, there is nothing very specific; I meant why were you hurrying up,' Pradeep explained and then asked, 'Vibha have you thought of going to conference?'

'Pradeep why are you asking, why don't you order that Vibha you have to accompany me to the conference in Pune!'

'Is it so? 'Pradeep grinned. 'So you are coming with me, in that case we would send the registration tomorrow and also accommodation charges. One room would do?' Pradeep winked.

'What! 'Her mouth was wide open, 'Pradeep we are not married yet.'

Then she changed the topic, 'Pradeep why don't you marry?'

'Marry to whom?'

'Marry to me! ''She shrieked.

Pradeep laughed. 'Hey don't laugh, I am serious about marriage, Pradeep, time is running fast, I am already thirty; don't want to be elderly primipara, you understand there are so many complications of pregnancy if mother is beyond 35 years of age.'

Finding Pradeep silent, she started,' Pradeep you never answer whenever I bring the topic of marriage for discussion.'

'Why are you in hurry to be married?' Pradeep asked.

She showed him the small fist, 'I will beat you.'

'How will you beat me?' Pradeep pricked her.

She sprang to her toes walked to him and beat with smaller of the fists. Pradeep kept on smiling.

'Ok, tell me what you will you like to take, hot or cold coffee?' Vibha asked.

'Hot will do,' Pradeep expressed his desire to drink coffee. Vibha walked to the kitchen to prepare coffee for him and her also.

Vibha was very serious about marriage he should not postpone it for long time, though he was not willing to marry to her, he did not want to lose her either. She was right in thinking because she was growing older and might have problems in pregnancy. But he did not want to marry her, he did not want to be hers he would marry to the girl who was beautiful, which she was not.

Vibha walked back to drawing with tray having two mugs of coffee, stretched her hand lifting one mug and gave it to Pradeep. 'Pradeep take it, I hope it is tasty.'

Pradeep stretched his hand to clutch the mug and held her fingers also, which quivered and the mug shook, coffee fell over her right thigh. 'Oh,' she winced and putting the mug on table ran to bath room to wash her burns with water, Pradeep followed her to the bathroom. She was pulling her sari up, when Pradeep came over there.

'Pradeep please go away, I have to wash it over there, upper part of thigh.'

'Let me wash it.'

'Hey, her eyes widened, it is upper part of thigh,' Vibha told him.

'So what, now you are my patient, let me see,' Pradeep reasoned.

'No please,' Vibha requested him to go away.

'Vibha don't behave as a child. Let me see where it is burnt.'

'Oh no, 'she was not in mood to allow Pradeep to examine the area as it was over the thighs, but she could not keep Pradeep away . . . It was second degree superficial burns and would heal with in ten days' time.' Pradeep told. 'I am so sorry, it had happened because of me; let me apply the ointment, and is there any ointment at home?'

'Soframycine must be there in the bedroom, on the side table, let me bring it.'

'I will bring,' said Pradeep and got to his toes to bring the ointment. He brought the ointment from the bed room and came to her.

'Give me the ointment I shall apply myself, 'Vibha demanded the ointment who had let the sari fall down over her legs.

'Let me apply,' Pradeep insisted.

'I will apply myself, 'she was stern.

Pradeep did not give her the tube of ointment, bent down and lifted her sari up and applied the ointment. While he was applying the ointment his index finger drifted little away from the burn wound towards the ecstatic valley, feminine valley. Vibha caught hold his hand and forcefully jerked that away.

'It is called misbehaviour Pradeep,' she retorted.

Pradeep grinned and straightened himself. 'I am so sorry, 'he was being galled.

'Go to the drawing I am just coming over there,' Vibha told.

Pradeep did not budge.

'Go,' Vibha rebuked finding him standing over there.

Pradeep walked over to the drawing. Vibha applied the ointment and sprang to her toes, as it was paining she went to the bed room and took out a Cambiflam tablet and swallowed the bitter pill with water.

Walking over slowly she came to drawing; coffee had become cold by then. 'I will make another cup of coffee, 'she said and lifted the tray. 'I will help,' Pradeep walked to kitchen behind her. She prepared two cups of coffee when Pradeep came over behind her, lowered his face a little bit so that she could feel the warmth of his exhaled air. It was so titillating, that even in those moments of agony, even in those moments of melancholy, she felt throbbing pulsations inside her, the valley, where Pradeep was trying to insert his finger and she had not permitted him to do so.

'Pradeep come, hold me crush me, I want to feel your hardness your stiffness . . . Come Pradeep.' She wanted to say but could not yell. Pradeep lowered his face further and put the lips over nape of the neck. The frission surged down, down over her breasts, her abdomen, and her thighs and over her feminine valley. Her whole body was electrified. 'Ah Pradeep! Ah!'

After some time she requested Pradeep to wait in the drawing, she would bring coffee over there in drawing.

She went to kitchen and holding the tray walked back to drawing. Pradeep lifted one mug and drank coffee out of it. Vibha was drinking coffee out of other mug, why Pradeep avoided the discussion about marriage. Might be he was shy of discussing the matter.

After finishing coffee she asked, 'Whether she should serve dinner. Everything was prepared except chapattis.'

'Vibha let us go to restaurant,' Pradeep suggested.

'Why?

'You are burnt, it would be so painful.'

'It's small burn; why are you so much worried, everything is ready and cooked we have to prepare the chapattis only. 'She got up and gave the newspaper to Pradeep to engage himself and walked over to the kitchen herself.

After cooking the chapattis she served dinner on the table and called Pradeep to come over to the dining. Pradeep walked to the table where Vibha had served the dishes.

The dinner was delicious and Pradeep praised her lot. Vibha was rejoicing her praise, might be then he agreed for marriage, but he did not yell a word for marriage. After dinner both strolled to the drawing and peered out at the star studded sky, seen in arts. Pradeep took her in arms.

'Pradeep I love you,' Vibha said, raking her finger over his chest, her right breast brushing against his chest writhing, caressing, and sending the frission of dalliance inside both bodies. They remained there for some time, and then separated.

'Let me go,' Pradeep said. Vibha grinned, 'Pradeep think of marriage.'

Pradeep came out of the door but she did not close the door on his back and kept on looking at back of Pradeep . . . 'Pradeep I love you,' she said slowly,' I love you Pradeep, I love you'.

Next day morning when Pradeep opened his chamber registrar came, 'Sir which case to be taken for operation first?' He asked.

'Same vaginoplasty patient is to be taken first, shift her to operation room and ask the anaesthetist to give her anaesthesia, I am coming, 'he told. Registrar turned to go when Pradeep called him; 'Listen, Dr Vibha had come?'

'I am here,' Vibha said entering the chamber at the same time.

'Oh you are here! Put on the sterile dress, patient is almost ready for operation,' Pradeep told her. She went to the ladies changing room. He also got up to put on the sterile dress.

The patient of vaginoplasty was shifted to operation room and was anesthetized. Ward boys have put her on lithotomy position. Pradeep went to operation room and scrubbed to put on the sterile gloves when Vibha also came. Pradeep came to operation table and marked the incision on the patient, he told the residents standing over there that he would do triple flap vaginoplasty which had been described for the first time by Dr Vishwa Prakash, a renowned Plastic surgeon from our own country. In this operation after creation of the space between bladder and rectum, two flaps of labia minora are harvested and applied inside the cavity. The main advantage of the operation is that the cavity which is created for vagina is not closed, which is a major drawback in any other operation. 'After teaching the residents he completed the operation.

After operation was finished he returned to the chamber, when he sighted Neelima sitting over there. 'You are Neelima, I suppose? 'He asked.

'Yes, and what about you? 'She asked flipping the mascara laden eye lashes.

Pradeep was lanced deep inside. 'I am Pradeep, Dr Pradeep.'

'Oh I am so sorry, could not identify you,' Neelima sprang to her toes and got up stretching her hand to shake his hand. The hand of hers were so soft, so sensuous, Pradeep's hand vibrated, his body vibrated and his whole body went on to powerful vibrations. 'Please sit down,' Pradeep offered the seat, ogling at her voluptuous breasts.

'I have read one of your article about raised lesions over the face and you treat these without scars. I am impressed by your work and want to get rid of my scars.' She explained pointing to her cheeks.

Pradeep came nearer to her and put his finger over her cheeks, 'Yes these lesions would heal without scars, 'he assured her.

'Doctor I have a doubt, doctors in my city told that there would be a line.'

'No in my procedure there is no line.' Pradeep again assured her.

'Is it so?' Neelima asked as she was not convinced.

'Yes, be assured that there would be no line,' Pradeep told her.

'Ok, then please do it, today.' Neelima demanded.

'Today! Neelima today the list was already prepared and you could not be adjusted,' Pradeep told 'Doctor do something, please do it today, 'she requested.

'Ok, there is one possibility; you may be operated in nursing home, if you wish so,' Pradeep suggested her way to get it done the same day.

'I don't mind if you operate in nursing home. Give me address, I will reach there.'

Pradeep gave her the address of nursing home and asked her to go there and be admitted. She got to her toes holding the paper over which the address was written and bading good bye came out of the chamber.

Vibha came in the chamber after finishing the dressing of the vaginoplasty patient.

'Is the patient shifted?' Pradeep enquired.

'Yes she is shifted out of operation room to recovery room,' Vibha told.

'You know what . . . .' Pradeep yelled. 'Neelima had come.'

'Neelima, who?' Vibha asked.

'Neelima—model, from Delhi.'

'Oh! For what?'

'She is having lot of acne scars over her cheeks for which she wants cosmetic surgery over the face.' Pradeep told.

'When are you planning to perform cosmetic surgery?' Vibha asked.

'In the evening,' Pradeep told.

'I shall also go with you,' Vibha told to Pradeep. He was not interested to take her along with him, but did not deny apparently.

He said, 'What will you do over there? It is cosmetic surgical operation.'

'I know, but even then I shall go with you, 'she retorted. How could I allow you to go to such beauties, you are my man, only mine . . .'

Why she was interested to go with him. He might caress her or kiss, or else . . . with her (Vibha) he won't be able do any dalliance activity, he grinned.

In the evening Pradeep did not take her along with him, and went alone to the nursing home.

'A patient, whose name is Neelima has been admitted, tell me the room no?' Pradeep asked the receptionist in the nursing home.

'Yes, sir she is admitted in room no 2,' receptionist told politely.

'Ok,' Pradeep walked to room no 2 and entered inside. 'How are you Neelima?' asked he.

Neelima sat on the bed, 'I am fine doctor.'

'Did you face any problem in locating the nursing home?' Pradeep asked.

'Didn't face much of the problems in locating the nursing home, it's well known nursing home; I could locate it very easily.'

'Ok, within 15 minutes I will call you in operation room. Nurse will come and give you sterile dress to put on, please change your regular clothes and wear sterile dress,' Pradeep told, his eyes could not avoid the sight of her protuberant breasts, jutting forward, wriggling inside the protective cotton wrap to come out . . . Pradeep felt sudden rush of the blood to his organs.

Nurse came with sterile dress and requested Neelima to put on. She inspected the dress and asked to the nurse, 'is it necessary to put on this dress, I am feeling little uncomfortable.'

'Madam it has to be put on,' nurse told her plainly.

Neelima put on the dress but it was really uncomfortable. She walked to the operation room in smaller steps holding the dress, lest it might slip from over her body.

Pradeep glanced at her-stunning beauty, blossoming like primrose; her sensuous body could be spotted in parts through the dress.

'Neelima, come to the operation table and lie down,' Pradeep requested Neelima to lie down over the table. She climbed over the flight of three steps to reach the operation table and turned to lie down, which caused her marvellous posteriors to be glimpsed at causing rush of extra blood to his manly organ which became stiff.

Neelima lay down over the table when Pradeep controlled himself and his raging primeval desire, aching for dalliance activity with her, draped her cheek and face with sterile clothes to start the operation.

He took 5 ml of Xylocaine in the syringe and diluted with normal saline to make it one per cent solution, injected slowly to make the cheek painless, rechecked for anaesthesia and when he was sure that anaesthesia was effective, started the cosmetic surgery. After operation, he told her that operation was over and she should rest in bed he would come next day morning and discharge her from the hospital. Neelima exulted. 'Is it so doctor, operation is over, I am so thankful to you doctor?'

Vibha was in bad mood in her apartment why Pradeep had not taken her along with him she was waiting for him to come and to take her along . . . slowly her anger melted into softness, oh Pradeep you should have taken me along with you, I would have assisted and helped you in operation.

In the morning Pradeep went to examine Neelima and discharged her. When he entered the room, Neelima was lying on the bed with eyes closed. Finding somebody entering the room she opened her eyes and saw Pradeep, when reedy smile crept over her luscious lips.

'Are you alright?' Pradeep fidgeted, 'something wrong?'

'No doctor, I am perfectly normal,' Neelima told him and sat on the bed.

'Are you feeling pain?' He asked.

'Not much, its tolerable. I had just taken pain killer tablets.'

Pradeep examined her wounds over the cheek and told her that she could go home if she desired so.

'When I have to come back for dressing?' she asked.

'After 7 days your dressing is to be changed,' Pradeep told her.

'Doctor you are great plastic surgeon, why don't you start your practice of plastic surgery in Delhi?' Neelima suggested to him.

'Pradeep glanced at her and said,' Neelima, everybody is born with certain cards, luck as it may be called. I am not well off financially so I have to settle in Aligarh.'

'Doctor, you are a great plastic surgeon for you there should not be a problem in settlement in Delhi. I will help you in settling in Delhi in plastic surgery practice,' Neelima grinned, her voluptuous breasts wriggled together, rising and falling and the cliff situated over the soft mountainous projections on was still more sensuous, she must be having well developed nipples, Pradeep developed sudden urge to feel and caress those nipples . . . . the nipples-tiny flesh surrounded by pink areola, as if a bee sitting over a pink petal of rose which would sting if touched; it always stings her bee would also sting if that is so he would like to be stinged how so severe pain it might produce.

'Neelima let us see what happens in future,' Pradeep grinned. 'Ok Neelima I shall inform the duty doctor to prepare your discharge ticket. Come on Sunday for change of dressing.' Pradeep told her and walked out of her room.

From nursing home Pradeep went directly to hospital and went to his chamber when Vibha entered, who was in bad mood. 'Pradeep where were you last night?' She was in anger.

'Last night I was at my apartment.'

'I have asked you to take me with you when you went to operate Neelima, why did you not take me?'

'Oh!' Pradeep pretended. 'I just forgot.'

'You did not forget intentionally did so. Why?'

'Vibha it is not necessary to take you everywhere along with me, 'he was irritated.

'Pradeep, do you understand what are you are saying, 'she squeaked.

'I understand madam Vibha,' he answered plainly.

'What do you understand?' She roared like a lioness.

'I understand what you are saying, but you should not behave in this manner with me, understand,' Pradeep said curtly.

'Pradeep,' her eyes were wide with frustration. And she turned to go out.

When she walked out, Pradeep was in gloomy mood. He should not have answered to her in such bad manner. For some time he kept on sitting in gloomy mood.

He took out the Operative surgery book written by Rob and Smith and tried to find out the procedure for incompetent cervix. But it was not detailed in the book. He had listened to the speech of Dr Vishwa Prakash about incompetent cervix . . . How to get the details of the procedure, he had to operate the next day. It was after noon lunch time, and he was in his chamber after taking the round of his operated patients.

Vibha entered the chamber; there was nothing reminiscent of the morning over her face. Pradeep was happy to find her in his chamber as he never believed that after his insulting behaviour to her she would come back to his chamber unless he apologised.

'Welcome Vibha,' he welcomed her.

'I have come, but don't think I have pardoned you.'

'I am so sorry for my behaviour,' Pradeep got to his toes and walked to her. He tried to take her in her embrace, when she frittered away.' No.'

Pradeep toiled hard to take her in embrace, he clutched hard so hard that her breasts were pinned against his chest.

'You are too fiendish man,' Vibha commented.

'Fiendish! I have not done anything like that to be called fiendish, it is bad adjective for a person like me, not suitable, 'he said and lowered his face to keep his lips over hers, but she turned her face away.

Chapter 2

Sunday morning was pleasant. Pradeep opened his eyes and glanced at the watch, it was seven in morning, he got up and sat on the bed. Neelima would come up for dressing that day at his apartment. He was mesmerized by her charm, it had never happened before to him. Was it lust which he should not develop for a patient. The relation of doctor and patient is very pious and there should not be any feeling of lust in between them but he was developing some feelings for her, lust or love, he did not know.

She was discharged on Tuesday and all through the five days he could not forget her, her mascara laden eye lashes protuberant breasts silky rounded posteriors, everything of her had reminded him of her. On Tuesday when Vibha asked him to take her with him for a movie, he refused. She was annoyed but he was in melancholy mood. Not able to feel anything, not able to enjoy anything as Neelima had enshrouded him with her charm radiating through every bit of her 5 feet 9 inches fleshy structure.

Neelima, neelima, Neelima; he had lost his identity to Neelima.

He slid out of the bed and walked to the kitchen to prepare morning tea, holding the mug filled with tea he strolled outside to verandah pulled out a chair to sit on that, keeping the legs over a stool. Chirping of birds was very pleasant, nature is always so soothing.

He wanted a girl like Neelima to marry. The wife of Plastic surgeon should be beautiful and smart and she had offered her help in his settlement in Delhi. It would be good for his future. Aligarh was not suitable place to settle. Dull, boring. A Plastic surgeon like him should settle in place like Delhi.

Putting the empty mug on the table, he lifted the newspaper, When Dr Maheshwari came. He was lecturer in medicine and was residing in the apartment next to Dr Gupta, whose apartment was just next to his, he was lecturer in anaesthesia, had been transferred from some other medical college and was posted in Gynaecology department.

'Good morning,' Maheshwari wished him and sat on the vacant chair lying over there.

'How are you?' Pradeep asked.

'I am fine.'

'How is the life?'

'As usual, dull and boring, 'answered Maheshwari.

'Maheswari, what is wrong with you, you are married to a beautiful girl of wealthy family . . .'

'How does that matter, Dr Pradeep?' Maheshwari put up a question.

Pradeep was puzzled, had no words to spell was under the impression that Maheshwari must be happiest doctor in the college; when he was married to Pratibha four years ago he was envious of him and his fortune. She was extremely beautiful rose of the garden of God . . . even more beautiful than Neelima.

He was well dressed by ten, when somebody knocked at the door. His heart skipped a heartbeat which started to pound at fast pace. He rushed to the door as if a second's delay might do something wrong opened the door and found Neelima standing over there, Neelima, clad in azure blue salwar suit was appearing a nymph. Upper part of the suit was carved at bosom to fit the bubbling breasts, which were thrusting suit to come out and be freed. He developed sudden salacious urge to caress her breasts, slowly and slowly.

'Come inside please,' he made the way for her to come inside. He had asked Neelima to come to his apartment for dressing just to avoid to go to nursing home for small dressing. And at apartment he would be able to talk to her, gloat at her and get glimpses of her, caress her breasts and further . . . . , further he did not know . . .

Neelima sat on sofa in the drawing; Pradeep closed the door and came back to Neelima, 'How are you?' Pradeep asked.

'I am fine,' Neelima opened her lips when her teeth sparkled like thunder in the sky, and surrounded by luscious inviting lips, inviting pradeep to caress with his fingers or lips.

'Ok I will change the dressing today, before dressing let us take something to drink, tell me what will you like to take, coffee?' Pradeep asked. She agreed for coffee.

Pradeep walked to the kitchen to prepare coffee for her. Neelima got to her toes, 'Nobody else in the house?' She enquired and walked inside the kitchen, 'Let me help you in preparation of the tea, or coffee. 'Are you unmarried?' She asked, helping him in putting coffee powder in the milk.

'Yes,' answered Pradeep. He was happy that he was unmarried.

'Why don't you marry?' Neelima just commented pouring coffee in two mugs which Pradeep has already kept over the platform.

'Searching for a suitable girl,' Pradeep told.

She giggled. 'Ok tell me what qualities are you looking at in your girl?'

'Beautiful, attractive and sexy body.'

'That should not be the only criteria, I suppose,' Neelima said lifted the tray with coffee mugs, and walked to drawing kept the tray over the table; lifted one mug to give to Pradeep and second for her.

'Like you,' Pradeep continued after pause.

Neelima blushed and then giggled, 'Am I beautiful and sexy?'

'There is no doubt in it, you are beautiful, gorgeous and have superbly sexy body.'

Neelima again laughed roaring. 'You are great, Dr Pradeep.'

After the coffee was finished Pradeep told her to come to the room for dressing he had changed one room of his apartment into the dressing room so that he had not to go every time to nursing home or the hospital. Neelima followed him to the dressing room. 'Neelima I am impressed by your behaviour,' Pradeep told her.

'I am also impressed by you, doctor,' Neelima praised him.

Pradeep asked her to sit on the dressing chair and removed dressing from over her cheeks, the result of surgery was spectacular, superb. 'Neelima, result is superb, no scar at all, look in the mirror.'

Neelima glanced in mirror, she was exulting, 'Oh I don't believe the result could be like this, no scar at all, am really thank full to you.'

Pradeep applied the ointment and did the dressing again after which she got up on her toes and straightening the crumpled salwar suit, thrusted her feet in the beautifully carved black sandals.

Pradeep asked her for the prescription Card which was given at the time of discharge from nursing home. 'Oh! it is in the hand bag in drawing,' she told and walked out of the room to drawing with swagger, her posterior protuberances arousing the primeval desires, desire to taste the nectar of blossoming youth, blossoming feminine beauty. She delved in bag to find out the prescription card and brought it out, gave that to Pradeep stretching her hand, who had also come in the drawing. Pradeep nibbled some medicines and told her that only one of the medicine had to be taken daily for 2 weeks.'

'What about other medicines which you had prescribed previously,' Neelima enquired moving her luscious lips, glossy and lipstick laden. Pradeep was imagining keeping his lips over hers and moving slowly, slowly, and slowly; and his masculine organ started to throb.

'What about other medicines doctor? 'She asked again.

'You should stop them all.'

She put the prescription card back in the bag and straightening her neck told Pradeep, 'I had discussed with one of my friend about you, he is having a big nursing home in Greater Kailash, agreed to give you a chamber for your plastic surgical practice. Visit some time. My address is with you just phone me whenever you have decided to come to Delhi I will make all arrangements from pick up from railway station to stay.'

Pradeep grinned,' I shall come however can't tell the date now. Give me some time and I will tell you over the phone.' Pradeep told her.

'That is perfectly alright, I shall wait for your call,' said Neelima moved her lips which were very much inviting, Pradeep longed to just touch them; but he could not.

Neelima did what he was longing to do, she put her lips over his and gave a powerful, sexy and soothing kiss; which instantly made him to vibrate with passion, and he clasped her, embraced her and put his lips inside her mouth.

After sometime Neelima bade him good bye and came out. Pradeep kept on looking at her with impudence, her firm rounded posteriors, jostling with each other; when she was no longer visible, Pradeep slammed the door and crawled to the bed room.

Her arrival and departure had passed as nightmare to him. Just few minutes back she was preparing coffee in the kitchen, and his apartment came to life, every inanimate thing became lively, the air inside became so pleasant as if it was caressing his body and giggling and then caressing her sensuous body. Apartment without a woman is dead, he thought for the first time and decided to marry, marry to whom? Vibha? Neelima? ?

Neelima had aroused the desire in him, passion in him for female body and she was the woman who had aroused the longing for female sexuality and the marriage.

Pradeep got to his toes and walked to kitchen, and slowly touched the mugs she held in her hand as if he was caressing the sensuous hand of Neelima, lifting the mug he put his lips on that as if he was caressing her cheeks and lips as she had done, she had kept her lips over his; the moment was to be cherished, the blissful moments have to be remembered. Why the time did not stop over there, why she was not here to remain in lip lock for ever, why she had gone away?

Neeilma my love, my love at first sight. He walked outside the kitchen following the foot marks of hers to the hall where she was standing with her lips over his.

Neelima I am mad in love for you. It is love or lust, whatever it is, I love you Neelima, Neelima I love you.

Walking to the window he peered out to find the sight of posterior protrusions of Neelima, but alas there was a cow only over the whole stretch of the street.

His sleep was disturbed by the sound of the ringing bell. Who could be at this hour, he glanced at his watch, Vibha . . . might be. He got to his feet and walked to the gate to open it. Vibha was standing over there.

'You are sleeping!' Vibha was surprised. Pradeep made the way for her to enter but did not move his lips, as he was not happy on her untimely arrival. 'Pradeep are you ill?'

'Slight headache.'

'Oh,' said Vibha and put her hand over his forehead. As she was putting her hand over the forehead she could sight the foot marks of sandals. 'Somebody has come?' She asked.

'One of the patients had come,' Pradeep told her casually without giving much importance.

'Special patient?' Vibha was intrigued, why he had called the patient at apartment.

Pradeep smiled. 'Neelima had come, 'he told.

'What!' She shrieked, 'Pradeep why have you called her at apartment? 'She was envious of her something seems to be between two of them. My man had been enticed by Neelima.

'Where else should I have called her?' Pradeep retorted.

'You should have called her in hospital or nursing home for dressing, not at apartment.'

'In this hour of day I would not have liked to go to hospital and that too on Sunday.'

'You should have called her on working day,' Vibha reasoned.

'Okay I would pay attention to it; I know that you are envious of her.' Pradeep told her. Then he changed the topic, 'Vibha is there something wrong with Maheshwari?'

'Hey don't change the topic,' Vibha was stern. 'If you call a woman patient over here, you have to tell me, okay my love,' Vibha told him.

Pradeep agreed to get rid of her anger at that time.

Love! The word love soothed her deep inside. Love, your love and my love . . . and she put her fingers over his hand, caressing through coarse hair which tingled her own body. 'Pradeep You should not call your women patients over here. Ok tell me what were you saying about Maheshwari?'

'Something is wrong with Maheshwari?'

'Why are you thinking so? 'Vibha asked.

'Maheshwari had come in the morning he was not in happy mood.' Pradeep told.

'Don't you know?'

'What?'

'Maheshwari is married to a beautiful girl of wealthy family, however she does not bother for him, and she is bad character girl too.'

'Bad character! What do you mean?' He asked.

'She visits Dr Gupta very frequently,' Vibha told.

'She visits to Dr Gupta!' Pradeep was surprised.

'Leave it Pradeep I am famishing let us go for lunch,' Vibha suggested but Pradeep was in no mood to go for outing. After meeting Neelima, he was completely lost in her and did not like to go anywhere or with any other girl, even if she was Vibha.

'Ok I should prepare lunch over here,' she proposed.

She got to her toes and walked to kitchen. She appeared ugly to Pradeep no prominent posterior, no slim waist Neelima was ecstatic . . . and at that moment of the time she appeared very ugly.

That is how primitive human instincts behave. Vibha was her friend and good looking, but when another girl came she appeared ugly though she was not ugly.

She was sure that Pradeep would marry to her. However he was in no mood to marry her and there was no reason to marry her. Neelima was superb, her protuberances have ignited him everywhere. Vibha could evoke some responses some times, but they were never so intense, he never developed such hard flesh at any time in his life, it remained so for long time, he just murmured, 'Neelima,' and again felt blood rushing to his masculine flesh.

Cluttering of the utensils was emanating from the kitchen. She was preparing the lunch, how much she loved him and it was the reason he was worried much, he did not want that her confidence was broken . . . Sometimes people take extreme steps to the extent of the suicide also, he shuddered deep inside.

Vinha returned with tray having two hot dogs and tea which she hurriedly prepared for lunch, she stretched her hand to give one to Pradeep and took other in her hand.

He thanked Vibha for tasty hot dog she had prepared for him. He was munching hot dog prepared by Vibha but lost in Neelima. If he practised in Delhi, he might become the Plastic surgeon of India fame and then Delhite girls would flock to him for plastic surgery. He had heard that Delhite girls were too advanced, while here in Aligarh there was no scope of cosmetic surgery. The only hitch was Vibha, if he settled in Delhi he had to marry to Neelima. Vibha wanted to marry him but she never allowed him to caress over her breasts. Now he was not interested in caressing her breasts Neelima's breasts were more protuberant and he would like to caress over them she would let him caress certainly. The protuberances of Neelima appeared affront and he cupped his hands as if he was cupping the soft flesh of hers.

He cast a glance at Vibha who was taking a bite at the hot dog,' Vibha I am planning to start my practice of Plastic Surgery at Delhi,' he spelled to know the reaction of Vibha to his proposal.

'This is good idea. In fact a Plastic surgeon of your repute should shift to Delhi, 'she agreed with him.

'Neelima had a meeting with one of her friend who was having his own nursing home, he had agreed to give one chamber to me for private practice.'

'It would be good as I am concerned, I would take employment somewhere or start my practice in Delhi.' Vibha told her plans.

'What!' he shrieked to himself she was planning to shift to Delhi with him, hey Neelima was there.

He looked at Vibha who had reclined in the sofa. 'Vibha you should be cautious,' Pradeep suggested.

'For what?' Viha asked.

'Some body might see us together,' Pradeep reasoned.

'Pradeep don't behave in childish manner, we are adults and going to be married,' Vibha quipped.

The words going to be married lanced him deeper inside; she was so determined and sure to be married. Lord, she was sure of their marriage. He had to explain that he wanted a beautiful girl in his life as his woman and not average looking girl like her.

'Pradeep I received a sms from my father that he was coming to Aligarh the next Sunday to meet you,' Vibha spelled to Pradeep.

'Meet me! Why, for what reason?' Pradeep asked pretending to be ignorant.

'Hey, to talk about marriage plans.' Vibha said tersely.

'Marriage plans!' He was lanced inside.' Marriage!' he stammered.

'But I am not in Aligarh on Sunday,' Pradeep told her, 'I am going to Delhi.'

'Why are you going to Delhi? 'She frowned upon her left eye brow raised.

'To visit the nursing home, Neelima had suggested and explore the possibilities of private practice of Plastic surgery over there in Delhi,' Pradeep explained.

'Change your plans, go to Delhi next to next Sunday, father had agreed after lot of persuation to come to Aligarh and have a word with you, 'she told Pradeep and requested to stay back on Sunday.

'Vibha I have already fixed everything with Neelima,' Pradeep persisted.

Vibha was visibly upset and irritated, 'I am fad up with Neelima, you will not go anywhere with Neelima next Sunday, 'she told him firmly.

Neelima had started haunting as ghost she was afeared of her. Pradeep had to be prevented from going to meet her, basic instincts are that if male and female meet frequently their primeval flow of sexual energy cant be prevented, his man was not like that before, Neelima had enticed him.

Pradeep did not say a word he was laughing deep inside, she was thinking that he would follow her advice. Now nothing could prevent him to go to Delhi and meet Neelima—his heart throb.

'Father shall fix the date for ring ceremony. I plan to be married this season,' Vibha told Pradeep.

Pradeep was jittery with vibha, she was planning for marriage while he was lost in Neelima, should he tell Vibha that he wanted to marry Neelima. How could he tell that Neelima had not shown inclination to marry him. He would marry Neelima and again the voluptuous boobs glittered in front of his eyes he had seen towering down while she was lying down on the operation table mere sight of which had made him to **ford in the river of sensuality** and he dabbled for long till the sister told him to take out injections xylocaine which he had to inject in the cheek of Neelima before operation.

'Vibha I am feeling tired as could not sleep the whole of the night, I will like to go to sleep,' Pradeep changed the topic.

'Pradeep don't change the topic. Listen you are not going anywhere the next Sunday. At present if you are feeling sleepy, go to sleep, I shall also sleep here in drawing,' Vibha told him sternly.

'Alright,' said Pradeep and strolled to the bed room. She lay on the sofa and was fast asleep immediately.

After some time she woke up and walked to bed room where Pradeep was asleep, she called him, 'Pradeep.'

Pradeep awoke and sat on the bed. 'Oh my God, slept for 3 hours,' Pradeep said glancing at the watch, he got to his toes. 'Pradeep wait in drawing I will prepare tea for you.'

Vibha walked to the kitchen to prepare tea for both of them, Pradeep walked to the drawing and thrust himself on the sofa wavering it. Next Sunday he would go to Delhi Neelima had invited him. But next Sunday was after 7 days. How would he live for seven days without having the glimpses of Neelima, glimpses of her beautiful bosom, beautiful lips, without kissing them . . . and a frisson of sensuality flew his body making him aflame, aflame of thinking of romp, yes romp he would not be able to endure missing Neelima for long, what to do . . . he was disconcerted . . . .

Coming to his toes he strolled to the window and peered out, fixing his gaze at the spot where he had spotted Neelima, where he could glance at her luscious firm and rounded hips, and kept on clinging the gaze at the spot, a plume rose and through the plume of excitement he could see Neelima over there; Just imagination of her artistically carved hips sent innumerable waves inside his body floppy organ to be throbbing and pulsating.

'Tea,' Vibha interrupted his thoughts holding the tray with two cups of tea in that. Pradeep turned and lifted cup walking back to the sofa holding his cup. Extremely beautiful girl, what a crabbed body, glow radiating from her body, gorgeous ideal shaped breasts, ideal shape described in the books, he had read in his Plastic surgical books the ideal shape of the breasts which should be achieved undergoing breast reconstructions, but never achieved, Ideal is to be described but is never achieved in medical science.

But Neelima had beautifully carved breasts as described in the books ideal shape indeed, though he had not seen her breasts or felt either without the protective wrap of cotton, but whatever he could see when she was lying on the table was enough to find out what was lying hidden behind protective covering, prodding forward as if to challenge the onlooker . . .

Imagination of her breasts made him restless again, sipping tea he casted a glance at Vibha, who was staring at him, 'What is the matter? You are very much disconcerted.'

He kept his empty cup on the table and kept on looking at her peeping in her eyes. How her eyes would look like if he broke the news that he was interested I Neelima and not in her that he wanted to marry Neelima and that he wanted to pierce her virginity with fierce act of sex. Was she virgin, might not be even if she was not he wanted to have insertion with ferocity inside her and not Vibha, in fact he could not make fierce relations with her make ferocious act like a rabid aimal, rabid man rabid and blinded by radiations of love radiating of sensuous body of his woman. Pradeep was lost in Neelima and suddenly his gaze slid from her face down on her bosom, her breasts were also well proportioned, but Neelima's breasts were ecstatic, which could arise the passion inside anybody make lively a floppy organ.

'Pradeep don't try to befool me, I know each and everything.'

'What do you know?' Pradeep asked sheepishly did she know he was lost in Neelima that he wanted to pierce her womanhood deep very deep inside that he was not feeling rush of blood to his limp flesh and that that was made stony hard by surge of blood rushing just by the glimpses of her feminine carvings at bosom.

'Everything,' she spelled plainly she knew that he was lost in Neelima and in her body which had made him mad for her.

'What?' Pradeep asked again at least she should spell what did she know.

'You are lost in that wench female,' Vibha parted her lips away from each other.

'Wench!what do you mean?'

'Neelima, the wench female.'

'Vibha,' he retorted, 'You should not speak in that way for a good woman.'

'Good woman!' she shrieked, 'She is good woman!'

Pradeep looked at her helplessly.

'She has enthralled you, enthralled of her charm, of her beauty, of her body; beware of such girls, otherwise . . . .'

'Otherwise . . . ?'

'Otherwise she will make you her doggy, 'she said and giggled.

In those gloomy moments also Pradeep could not avoid smiling at her comments.

'Huh,' said Pradeep carelessly and walked to his bed room, Vibha looked at him through the corners of her eyes.

Neelima had smothered my Pradeep, she should be careful else she would lose him. These girls always believed in eating, drinking and be merry; while my man was very innocent. No doubt she was beautiful and men are always enthralled by the beauty of women. It is males 'weakness, and not the fault of Pradeep in any way. However it was her duty to save him from the clutches of feminine charm of Neelima . . . Pradeep should not go to Delhi next Sunday . . .

If he did not agree to her advice, he might refuse, he was mesmerized by her luscious lips, or prodding breasts, she thumped her forehead with the heel of the palm; she should go with him.

Pradeep returned back to drawing putting on explicit dress, 'Vibha let us go somewhere; I am feeling bored,' he suggested.

'Oh!' Vibha giggled, 'looking handsome, 'she was in ecstasy as it was first offer in her life time from Pradeep. 'Thank you Pradeep' she said and got to her toes.

'Thanks for what?' Pradeep just spelled.

'Alright, 'she said getting up and walked to the door, 'I have to change these clothes, shall go and come back within no time; or you can come with me to my apartment.

Pradeep was in no mood to go to her apartment, but he got up presuming that change of the apartment might provide solace from the reminiscences of Neelima. in this apartment everything had become engrossed in her, sofa where she sat, kitchen where she prepared tea, and floor where she left the foot prints, not only that, the air of apartment was filled with aroma of her body . . .

Change of the apartment would change the air filled with scent of Neelima, so he followed Vibha to her apartment.

'Wait here, I am coming,' once inside the apartment Vibha asked him to wait in drawing and without waiting for his answer walked to her bed room to put on fresh clothes.

'I am coming with you, 'spelled Pradeep, narrowing outer of his eyes.

'Where?' Vibha frowned upon.

'In the bed room,' he said plainly.

'What!' her eyes were wide, blood rushing to her cheeks she could feel the pulsations of blood rushing to her cavern, feminine cavern.

'You can come to my bed room after marriage,' she said turned back to him coming closer to him clutching his hand requested, 'Pradeep please don't go to Delhi next Sunday and meet my father . . . I want it to be done as early as possible.'

'I will try,' Pradeep said plainly.

'No try,' she squeaked, 'You have to stay back on Sunday in Aligarh', she said and walking over went to the bed room. How to persuade him and took him out of clutches of Neelima. She had made a mistake, on that evening, when Pradeep had not come to take her, she should have gone to the nursing home . . . One should be careful in these relations. Women is the weakness of men and she should have been careful. She had not thought that the situation would take a turn like that.

Pradeep sat on the sofa and lifted a magazine kept on the table. In the morning Neelima was sitting just infront of him, and she asked, what qualities he was looking in a girl to be his wife and he said she should be beautiful like her when she had blushed, he could feel the blood vessels pulsating beneath her skin as her breasts became more protuberant. Why she had blushed? Was she interested in him. If she would not agree for marriage, he would remain unmarried throughout the whole of the life.

Vibha came back clad in azure blue salwar suit. 'How am I looking?' She asked.

Pradeep gave trifling smile, 'Fine, beautiful.'

'Let's go,' said Vibha and came out of the apartment closing the door behind her. She was in high spirit for Pradeep had offered the outing which had never happened. Pradeep unlocked the car and sat on driver's seat. Vibha entered into the car from other side.

At the restaurant only one table was vacant at the far end, both strolled to that and occupied the seat over there. Reveried waiter appeared for the order and put the menu card in front of them.

After dinner Pradeep was a bit relieved of the boredom or the reminiscences of Neelima.

Back in the apartment Pradeep sat on the sofa stretching his legs on the table . . . and Neelima again haunted him.

Beautifully carved breasts of Neelima again haunted him, she was flipping her eyelashes as if a bird flipping her wings to fly high in the sky, the mascara laden long eyelashes as if flipping the pages of the book, unable to find a page from where to start, yes unable to find a place from where to start reading Neelima, her raven black long hair, inviting wide eyes, sharp and prominent nose and her beautifully carved out prominences over her bosom; from where to start reading? From where to start search for the sensuality of her body; eyelids nose or lips, he should start from lips going down or mountain up every inch of the skin was to be explored.

Her bosom, he had already thought many a times, were ideally shaped, having the natural peel of white glistening skin, over which his palm or fingers would have slipped when he was keeping his palm over her left breast, cupping it and then holding the prodding nipples in between index finger and the thumb caressing slowly to increase the stiffness further, jet black nipples against the background of white glistening skin of the breasts appeared as if a black fly had sat on the white flower or the black drop applied over the cheek of a beautiful girl to avoid the gaze and the evil eye. He suddenly twanged the nipples in fantasy and Neelima shrieked, in ecstasy, in pleasure and she became salacious, he twanged the teats again to take her to the frenzied world of ecstasy; when he opened the eyes, it was eight in the evening.

He had not caressed the nipples of any woman, not even of Vibha, not seen even, not talking of the patients; patients are patients and relations between doctor and the patient are pious, not seen the nipples of his woman, though he could see the nipples of Neelima . . .

Somebody knocked at the door. 'Come in,' Pradeep asked one to come in.

'Took the round?' Pradeep asked.

'Yes, ansrwered Vibha and walked to sit on sofa. As she sat the gaze of Pradeep wandered to her bosom, not as attractive as that of Neelima, he got up and strolled to stand behind her with intent to see towering down over her breasts and also the nipples . . .

Vibha looked at him, 'What happened?' She asked.

'Nothing.' he yelled keeping both his hands over her shoulders. Suddenly his left hand slipped over her bosom, Vibha immediately caught hold of his hand.

'Pradeep,' she squeaked.

'I am sorry, 'he was disconcerted at the incidence, he actually did not intend to that, hand slipped unintentionally, he was in remorse. 'I am extremely sorry, 'said he. Vibha controlled raging anger inside her body. But why she was so angry, he was her man, would not only caress her breasts but her feminine cave also, she thought and at the same time bethought the masculine and ecstatic touch of masculine hand over her breasts for the first time in her life. Skin of her breasts was throbbing as if to pulsate and be torn . . . In frenzied attack of ecstasy she closed her eyes.

When Vibha opened the eyes, she got to her feet and straightened the wrinkles from over salwar suit.

'Pradeep I am going now, 'she said.

'Where?' Pradeep asked. 'Where is hurry to go?' Pradeep was remorseful. 'Some work?'

'I have to go. You is more interested in Neelima—the wench, she has seduced you; you are not agreed to postpone the Sunday visit to Delhi.'

'Vibha,' Pradeep strolled nearer to her, clutched her hand and pulled, 'Come sit down, if you will go who would cook the dinner for me.'

'I am not going to cook dinner, 'she purred. 'I am not your wife, when I will be your wife shall prepare the dinner for you, then it would be my responsibility. At present I am your guest, cook food for me,' she spoke in whim wham grinning,' Or else, call Neelima, and order her to cook the dinner for you, when she would make you to cook food for her, then you would realize that such women are not to be good wives. But all males are the same, womanizers, found a beautiful woman and started walking behind her like a pet dog,' she said and giggled.

Chapter 3

Pradeep unlocked his chamber in the morning when registrar came, 'Sir would you come for round of the operated patients now or should I come later some time?' he asked.

'How are the patients?' he asked putting his bag on the table.

'They all are fine, I have seen all patients; the patient of vaginoplasty was enquiring when her dressing would be changed, I have told that it would be changed on Friday.

He told registrar that he would be coming for the round alongwith him.

On the way to the ward he met Dr Gupta who was talking to a nurse, Pradeep was amused, what had happened to this doctor. He should maintain his standard, the nurse was bad character, being celibate, she was having copper T in her uterus, he detected by chance when she had come to casualty for treatment of pain in loin he suspected it of kidney origin and advised an x ray, copperT being opaque was detected on X ray. People told that she was bad character call girl.

Was she seducing Dr Gupta, if that was so, he should be cautious, as his apartment was just adjacent to his apartment.

Pradeep hurried to ward, when nurse came for taking the orders for the patients. It was his OPD day, he ordered few of the patients to be discharged so that dated patients could be admitted.

After completing the round of the patients he came to his chamber when Vibha also came.

'How is the vaginoplasty patient?' She asked.

'She is alright, dressing would be done on Friday,' Pradeep told sitting on the chair, 'I will complete the research paper today,' Pradeep told.

'What about Sunday? What have you decided?' Vibha asked frowning, whatever might happen, she won't allow him to go to Delhi. She knew the males, all are same no difference in Gupta or Pradeep when it is related with women.

She was after him it wont be easy to go to Delhi but he had to go, Pradeep thought casting a glance at her, plain woman no flipping of mascara laden eye lids while Neelima 's flipped deeper into his heart and competed with flipping of heart beats when he missed many beats. 'Sunday!'

'Yes what have you decided to go to Delhi?'

'I am going to Delhi, I have already told you,' Pradeep was stern.

'Pradeep don't be stubborn, you can't go to Delhi, if you would persist then I would also accompany with you, 'she retorted.

'What will you do over there?'

'What you will do?' she counter questioned.

'Cosmetic surgery.'

'I shall assist you in cosmetic surgeries,' she said and raised her left eyebrow.

Pradeep smiled timidly and got to his toes, 'I have got to go to OPD Vibha.'

'You go anywhere but remember, you are not going to Delhi or I shall accompany you, 'she told her decision and walked out of the room with Pradeep. She turned away to her department while Pradeep turned to right to go to OPD.

On the way to the department she met Dr Gupta.

'Hello madam,' Dr Gupta wished her. 'Good morning. Going to the department?'

'Yes. 'She said plainly.

'I am also going to the Gynae department,' Gupta told.

'Come,' Vibha invited him without waiting for him to start.

Gupta followed her, she did not like him, 'Woman hunter always gloats at the women.'

'Are you single?' She asked Gupta walking with him.

Vibha did not yell a word, did it matter to him, was he prospective bridegroom, she giggled in herself; might be he thinking to make her his prey.

'Come to my apartment,' he invited her. Vibha did not intend to answer, as department had arrived she turned to enter inside.

Pradeep admitted two patients from OPD—one female patient had come for reconstruction of areola over her reconstructed breasts, other patient had come for labiaplasty; her labias were very much enlarged and were not aesthetically good looking, as she was a nude model she wanted to have aesthetically pleasant looking labia. Not only the aesthetic part, during sex the labias used to be traumatized. She was from Delhi and heard a lot about Pradeep so came for reduction labia plasty. One patient was admitted in male ward who was suffering with impotence.

After OPD Pradeep returned to his chamber and kept the kettle on the heater to prepare the tea, Vibha must also be coming as a routine so he was planning to prepare tea for her also. How to deal with this girl. She was bent upon going with him to Delhi which he never wanted, but there was no way by which he could avoid her going with him. Suddenly Pradeep developed urge to get glimpses of Neelima.' Ah! Her beautiful carved protrusions!!'

Vibha entered into the chamber. 'You are at the right time, tea is prepared,' Pradeep told her while pouring the tea in two cups. 'Tomorrow I shall perform an excellent operation,' Pradeep told to vibha.

'What operation?'

'Labia plasty.'

'Labia plasty!'

'Yes, the operation is done for enlarged labia.'

'Hey don't talk nonsense, labia are never enlarged,' Vibha argued with him.

'Your mentality is of a typical gynaecologist, she is having big labias which are not only unsightly but result in chaffing during sex.'

'Ok, how will you describe enlarged labia,' Vibha asked.

'If labia minora hang passed majora, condition is called hypertrophic labia' Pradeep told to her.

'And how are they enlarged?' Vibha queried.

'Usually it is since birth; at times it may be due to masturbation.'

'Due to?' asked Vibha as she could not hear the last words.

'Masturbation,' he told grinning.

'Huh,' she made the faces.

'There is another patient for reconstruction of areola.'

'Pradeep you always get such types of patients for operation, why?'

'I am genital reconstructive surgeon so I get such patients.'

'How will you reconstruct the areola? 'Asked Vibha coming to her toes and walking to the sink to keep the empty cup as she had finished tea.

'I shall reconstruct areola by labia minora,' told Pradeep.

'Pradeep why are you after female genitalia?' Vibha asked.

He smiled, 'I am one of the few genital plastic surgeons in the world.'

'Really!' she exclaimed.

'Yes.'

'I will like to see both of the operations,' Vibha requested.

'Come tomorrow in the operation room,' Pradeep agreed.

In the evening, Pradeep was feeling bored, he went upstairs to the roof, sun was shining mildly, crawling to hide behind the trees, he sat on the parapet and peered out. Suddenly he spotted the place where Neelima had turned to go away still remembering the cute evections covered by pink skin just like rose attracting herds of the bees, wasps and also the human beings.

How her areola would look like, he imagined, pink? Must be, and the nipples? Must be soft but could be made harder. Sun was no longer visible when he started to stroll on the roof, suddenly he heard the sounds of woman chuckling in the apartment of Gupta. Who could be the woman, Pradeep looked down in the apartment cautiously and found the same nurse sitting and talking to Gupta, she was in his arms who was disrobing her of her bra.

That was bad, Gupta should be prevented, Pradeep was strolling and thinking the ways and means to teach him a lesson, but what would he achieve, he (Gupta) might be after him causing troubles, he might say that he had seen women in his apartment too. That was wrong to call a nurse at apartment, but Neelima coming to his apartment could also be seen suspiciously.

Pradeep got down without caring for Gupta.

He walked to bed room and tidying the bed sheet took out a book in which the procedure of labiaplasty was described. When he turned the pages of the book, Neelima appeared, flipping her eyes leashes, showing her luscious inviting lips, grinning at Pradeep, inviting him to come to caress her lips. 'Pradeep come,' she yelled and smiled. Putting a book mark he closed the book and lost in Neelima.

She was really superb, it would be too ecstatic to kiss her, kiss at her luscious and libidinous lips, juicy indeed, and then lowering his lips down over her protrusions and over her raven black nipples; and his body twitched in agony of sensuality.

He sat on the bed; knees bent and face over the knees, 'Neelima you are mine, I love you.'

Pradeep unlocked his chamber in the morning when the registrar came and informed that the patient of labia plasty had been shifted to operation room.

'OK, ask the anaesthetists to give anaesthesia, I am changing my clothes to sterile gown and coming soon. Dr Vibha has come? 'He asked.

'She is already in the operation room.'

Pradeep washed his hands and came to operation room to perform the operation, he made the incision on the outer aspect of the labia and completed the operation, the whole operation took only 15minutes. When he finally stitched, he showed to all resident standing over there, the ideal shape and size of the labia minora which a woman should have.

He removed the sterile gown after operation and asked registrar to shift other patient for areolar reconstruction, Pradeep had to take a piece of labia minora and apply at the apex of the reconstructed breasts to simulate areola.

After the operation Pradeep came to his chamber where he found an envelope containing two registration forms from Fem Gen Con, lifting the envelop he entered the operation room again to find Vibha who was coming out of changing room.' Vibha two registration forms have been received, take one of the form, fill and apply for the permission from the government to attend the conference. He stretched his hand to give one form to her.

She clutched the form and turned to go to her department. 'I shall come in the evening and discuss,' she told and walked away.

Pradeep was lost in Neelima. He had asked Vibha to join him to conference, it would have been nice if Neelima would have accompanied him. Ah Neelima!Your protrusions, like a canto, what about the whole Neelima if canto is so thrilling, the whole poem would just kill him; and mere thoughts of long poem ending in canyon caused rush of blood to his masculine flesh, which started to harden.

In the evening Vibha walked to his apartment and sat reclining on the sofa, 'Pradeep I have talked to my HOD she had forwarded my application,' she told.

'Very fast,' Pradeep praised her.

'Yes I am always fast,' Vibha commented.

Neelima was sitting at the same place where Vibha was sitting. He had seen her artistic feet, whose nails were liberally smeared with nail polish. Sight of her feet was maddening and Pradeep had felt tingling all over his body, he had ascended his glance from toes to the dorsum of feet, to legs, thighs and to the cavern, and suddenly he was aroused intensively, a feminine small celibate cavern . . .

However feet of Vibha were ugly, messy nails, black. 'Vibha why don't you take care of your feet?' Pradeep told her to take care of her feet.

'What is wrong with my feet? 'She asked looking at her feet.

'You should keep the feet tidy and apply the nail polish.'

'Pradeep, you had never objected to my feet before, Oh, Neelima had applied nail polish?' She asked.

Pradeep did not answer, Neelima was Neelima and she was nowhere closer to her, Pradeep thought.

Vibha looked at Pradeep who was sitting with his eyes closed, she was disconcerted and rose to her feet, walked to window and peered out.

Medico girls were returning back to their hostel, she heard their chuckling and grinning.

Suddenly she felt that she had grown older, unmarried old celibate, Pradeep was not marrying her, his popularity was increasing, some other girl might seduce him; Neelima had intruded in his life from nowhere. She did not know what Pradeep thought about her, but signs were not good; she was modern girl and all males are alike, can be easily seduced by younger girls. For such women bond of marriage had no value, they get done what they wish, their feminine need is easily fulfilled by not one but many. Their valley was like big cauldron which could boil the liquids, a lot of liquids, in many men at one time. What to do? Pradeep was innocent and simple; she looked at him, sitting with closed eyes. She walked to him and kept her palm over his forehead.

He was irritated, 'What is the matter?'

She felt insulted and suddenly saline water filled her eyes a drop of which fell over his forehead.

'I am sorry,' Pradeep realised his folly.

'Pradeep,' she came in his embrace, 'I love you Pradeep,' She put her lips over his cheeks and exploring slid to lips. 'I love you Pradeep.' The saline water was pouring down which made Pradeep overwhelmed and he took hold of her.' I love you Vibha, I love you . . . 'He kissed her as if wanting to explore her lips, his lips sliding down over her neck and then over her nipples, when she insinuated her hand between his lips and her breasts. 'Pradeep this whole body is for you . . . let us complete the formalities of marriage, I am all for you.'

After sometime she parted away and wiped the tears sodden cheeks with her hand.

Chapter 4

Pradeep opened the door of his chamber and sitting on the chair waited for registrar to come as they had to go for the round of the operated patients. As he did not come Pradeep was restless, there must be something wrong, otherwise he was very sincere doctor.

Registrar came after some times panting for the breath, 'Sorry sir.'

'Why are you late? Did you face some problem?' Pradeep asked.

'I had to go to railway station,' he told.

'You had to go railway station, for what, to receive some guest?'

'Yes sir,' he agreed.

'To whom?'

He did not answer immediately, his cheeks were warm due to sudden rush of the blood. 'My fiancé, sir,' he told sheepishly.

Pradeep burst in laughter, 'Why are you shy then?'

He did not answer.

'Where is she?' Pradeep enquired.

'She is in the hostel.'

'Foolish fellow, go back to the hostel and you need not to come back today. Enjoy the moments with her lovely moments of your life,' Pradeep unofficially sanctioned one day leave to him.

He was nervous, and was unable to make up his mind whether to go or not.

'Sir you would go for the round of the patients?' He asked.

'I shall take the round with nurse you should go now.'

Registrar went away, Pradeep smiled to himself, who is his fiancée—Vibha or Neelima . . . ?

Getting on his toes he took out the apron from the rack and went to ward to see the postoperative patients. Nurse came for taking the orders, 'Sister I will do dressing of vaginoplasty patient, arrange for dressing trolley,' Pradeep told her to arrange for the dressing of the patients.

'Ok sir,' she went to bring the trolley and arranged everything. Pradeep opened the stitches and removed the mould which was kept inside the space he had created which was well maintained flaps of labia were well taken up. After cleaning the space he put the mould again.

'Everything is healed, you would be discharged in a day or two,' he told the patient. Coming back to his chamber he called the impotence patient to come to his chamber.

In the chamber Vibha was waiting for him.

'You are late today, I am waiting since long? 'She commented.

He cast his glance at the watch, 'Oh, 12 noon, today I had sent back my registrar to the hostel as his fiancée had come and the foolish fellow was wandering in the hospital.'

'Sensible you have done a sensible act today,' Vibha commended him.

'I am always sensible,' Pradeep said raising his right eyebrow.

'No, I don't agree to you as you are not at all sensible in the matter of our relations and marriage.'

Pradeep laughed. 'Marriage!' Then he changed the subject,' Vibha I had changed the dressing of the vaginoplasty patient, it is healed.

'You had taken the photograph?' She asked.

'Yes, and now I shall prepare the presentation today for the conference,' Pradeep told.

Somebody knocked at the door, Pradeep called him in. He was the impotence patient whom he had called in his chamber to do artificial erection test on him to find out the exact cause of his problem.

In the evening Vibha came in his apartment. Pradeep was in the drawing, he welcomed her.

'I was feeling bored, same routine from morning to evening. Patients and operations.'

Vibha looked at him, 'After marriage everything would be alright,' she comforted him.

'Marriage is not the answer for all the problems. Life may become even more miserable after marriage,' he drawled.

Vibha giggled, 'Our life wont be miserable, we would lead a happy life.' Suddenly she remembered,' Pradeep yesterday Maheshwari had fight with his wife.'

'Why?'

'Same matter.'

'What?'

'Extramarital affairs like congo, a dance when everybody dances at the tune following the leader and here leader is feminine body, his wife who is beautiful and a leader; Gupta and not only he dances with her, what beautiful dance it must be.'

'With Gupta?'

'Yes.'

'My God, how does he seduces the women, simple man, nothing extraordinary about him, but women are flocking to him, I am envious of him,' Pradeep commented.

'Nurse Sheela is a well kown bad character woman her frequenting Gupta is awkward but wife of Maheshwari visiting him is surprising. She is well educated woman, double MA from Agra university, was a lecturer in a degree college before marriage how she could be his prey. Pradeep was in remorse.

'Repenting?' Vibha giggled. 'Sometimes possibility of being beaten up by sandals should not be forgotton, you are balding already, after sandal beating you will become completely bald,' she retorted. 'All the males are same, drawling for female body. She had gone to Gupta's apartment while Maheshwari was asleep. When he woke up he did not find her he searched for her; and did not find anywhere. Suddenly he realized where she could have gone and lie on the bed again pretending that he was asleep. As soon as she jumped from Gupta's apartment and enterd the room to lie over the bed he caught her.'

'What did he say to his wife?' Pradeep asked.

'Nothing, he could not say a word rather she retorted,' Why are you awake at this hour?'

Pradeep cast a glance to find the facial lines over her face. She was friendly with him since first year of MBBS fifteen years passed since then must have kissed her merely 15 times or less but not more, she never allowed him to touch her boobs or go further down.

'Drawbacks of marrying the beautiful girl have to be faced by husband,' Vibha commented.

Pradeep was disconcerted, was she referring to Neelima.

'Don't you agree?' Vibha asked.

'Beauty should not be the sole criteria for the marriage. Girl should be considerate and good natured, a loving considerate girl proves a better wife. Beauty is ecstatic, ignites your passion but may not help in marital life.'

'What had happened to Pradeep, that wench varley woman had caused havoc to my man, she had pollulted him,' she was in melancholy mood. After some time she got to her toes and came out. Pradeep called her, but she did not listen.

He went to window and peered out, she could be spotted exactly on the same spot where Neelima had turned and he had got her glimpses, glimpses of her shapely rounded protrusions, inviting to caress them; while hers (Vibha's) posteriors were ugly, woman should have florid inviting posteriors, invite for dalliance activity between them . . . and man shuld feel his limp and floppy organ full with extra flow of the blood when he sights a woman walk with her back to him.

On Thursday morning Pradeep went early to the hospital as registrar had gone in leaves so he went straight to the ward and asked nurse to come to take orders. He took round of all the patients. Labiaplasty patient and patient of areolar reconstruction were alright. He asked the vaginoplasty patient to be discharged and asked the nurse to arrange for dressing trolley as he would do dressing of few patients.

First dressing was of labia plasty patient, he removed the dressing and found all stitches well healed, and the shape given to the labia was excellent. He took a photo graph.

Then he hurriedly took the round of the patients in male ward and came back to his chamber. Vibha had not come, he started missing her. He got to his toes, walked out of the room to the Gynae department to cajole Vibha.

She was in her chamber when Pradeep entered. 'Vibha,' he called her attention, 'Are you annoyed?'

She straighetend her face and looked at him.

'No, she said plainly twitching her lips.

'Vibha!' Pradeep called her finding her ignorant to his presence over there.

'Pradeep take this paper, I have got permission to attend the conference, now let us prepare for it.' Vibha stretched her hand to give him sanction letter from the government.

'Vibha!' he retorted, 'What is this?'

'What happened? Why are you so much angry? ?'

'Why did you not come today to my chamber?'

'Pradeep we should not meet very frequently.'

'Why?'

'Two persons of the opposie sex should not meet frequently and further I am not very beautiful, beautiful like Neelima.'

'Vibha are you mad? Come for tea, I am preparing,' he said and went out of her chamber.

Vibha was in no mood to go to his chamber, but Pradeep had called her, his man had called, how could she refuse, her anger became fluid and flew out of her eyes as saline water; wiping the tears she got to her toes to go to his chamber.

Why had he insulted her she had been his friend, had been friend and not only that she was a woman too, soft hearted, he should not have misbehaved with her in unmodest way or he would lose her, Pradeep was disconcerted. When Vibha came, Pradeep took her in his arms and put his lips over hers. Suddnely the saline water started flowing over both cheeks and met with one another, the anger flew away.

Vibha came in the evening to the apartment of Pradeep where he was putting the application form and summaries of paper to be presented at Fem Gen Con at Pune in an envelop.

'What are you doing Pradeep?' she asked meekly.

'Preparing the enevelop for the Fem Gen Con.'

'Have you not sent yet?'

'No, I shall send it tomorrow.'

Vibha sat on the sofa opposite Pradeep. 'Pradeep I have not asked you in the morning about patients of labiaplasty and areolar reconstruction, how are they?'

They are fine, 'I had seen the dressing of both the patients in the morning and they were doing well.'

'Plastic surgeons are great,' Vibha commented.

'What made you think so?' Pradeep asked.

'They carve a body, an organ and reconstruct, thrilling. Plastic surgeons are the artist doctors,' Vibha put up her point.

He laughed. 'You are right,' then after pause he enquired, 'Vibha how is your wound? Let me see.'

'What!' her eyes were wide. There is no need to see, 'she rebuked. 'Everything is alright.'

'But even then I wanted to see,' Pradeep persisted.

'No need,' she retorted. 'Pradeep,' she said after wards, 'I am longing for tea.'

'Make it, go to kitchen and make for me also.'

'You are ordering me as if I am your wife,' she said getting on her feet.

On the way to kitchen her saree got stangled in the dining table and she fell, sustaining sprain of ankle,' she shrieked In agony.

'What happened?' Pradeep rushed.

'I just fell down, ah! it is paining.'

Pradeep examined her. 'Sprain,' Prdaeep spelled, Vibha looked at her helplessly.

'Don't worry,' he supported her to get up so that she could rest on the bed, from bed room he brought painkiller tablets and gave one to her with water. She swallowed the tablet and lay over the bed. Pradeep brought out a crepe bandage and walked to Vibha,' I will tie the crepe bandage,' Vibha agreed.

He shifted the saree up.

'Hey what are you doing?' She shrieked.

'Cool down, I am just tying the bandage.'

'You have lifted my saree so high up, why, for what reasons?'

Pradeep shifted her saree further up above knee which Vibha caught immediately and pulled down below knee. 'Pradeep, rascal, you can tie the bandage without lifting my saree.'

Pradeep laughed. 'Why are you afeared of me?'

'Every women has to be afeared of men, you are not my man till marriage; once marriage takes place, then you can lift saree as high as you want.'

'How much high? Just show me.'

'Pradeep,' she again shrieked.

'You cant lift my saree, even if marry to me, it does not give you right to bare me.'

'Yes why to raise the saree up, when you should remove it,' Pradeep made the sarcastic comment.

'Pradeep!' she whimpered.

'Ok, I will not raise it,' assured Pradeep and tied the crepe bandage, after which he caressed her leg, which was silken and smooth. Initially Vibha did not realize but when his hand reached high over the thigh, her eyes were wide, 'cheat.'

Suddenly both of them burst in laughter.

Like previous day on Friday also Pradeep went early to the hospital and straight to the ward for round of the patients admitted over there, as all the dressings were done the previous day, not much of the work was left behind for that day. He called the sister and dictated the orders of all the patients who were to be posted for surgery on the Saturday.

Vibha had applied leaves for 7 days for she was not able to walk and gave the application to Pradeep. He went to the department of Gynae after the round to submit the application in the office.

After handing over the application of the leaves to clerk over there in the office he went to the apartment of Vibha, she was in her drawing in night dress, her pink night gown was ecstatic through which her breasts were discernible. Pradeep ogled at boobs through the protective wrap and his glance stopped at one point where small protrusion of flesh could be sighted, must be nipple, should he caress it, little bit. Finding Pradeep ogling at her bosom she retorted,' Pradeep, you are ogling at me, bad manners, and then realizing that her night gown was too transparent she dcided to put on suitable day time dress. She got to her toes to go to put on suitable day time dress but felt pain and again sat down, she shrieked in agony.

'What happened? What you need?' Pradeep asked.

'Nothing,' she retorted, 'Why are you ogling at my bosom, bad manners, I would change this dress. Go inside and bring my saree.'

'Why?'

'For wolf like you.'

He laughed roaring.

'I will not bring saree, you are looking sensuous in this dress,' he walked to her and stood behind her lowered his mouth to gave her a kiss.

'But no further,' she rebuked him.

Padeep laughed, 'Ok I will prepare tea for you.' Pradeep went to kitchen, Vibha reclined on the sofa where she was sitting. He came back with tray having two cups of tea when she tried to sit straight which resulted in pain. Pradeep came for help and sat on her side put his hand over back supporting her to get up. As she was trying to sit his hand slid over her left breast.

'Pradeep,' she retorted, 'Take it away.'

'What?'

'Hand.'

'Which hand?' he asked innocently and caressed her boob slowly.

'Pradeep!' she sat up and caught hold of his hand.

After tea, Pradeep walked back to hospital entered his chamber and pulled out a book As he was going through the book, a lady entered holding a X-ray in her hand accompanied by another lady.

Pradeep looked at them and asked, 'What can I do for you?'

'I want to consult for microsurgial tuboplasty,' Lady said holding X-ray.

'For how many years you are married?' enquired Pradeep waving at them to take the seat.

'Five years,' she answered.

'In such cases first thing to be done is laparoscopy,' looking at x-ray he explained, 'As your tubes are blocked, laparoscopy is to be done.'

'Alright, so what is the procedure?'

'Come to OPD tomorrow and from there you would be admitted.'

'Alright thank you very much.' They thanked him for kind and nice words and got up to go.

In the evening Pradeep brought packed dinner for them. It was nine in the evening, he peered out and saw Maheshwari disembarking from the ricksaw. Suddenly he remembered the sentence spelled by Vibha 'beautiful girls are always source of misery for men.' He did not agree at that time, but later on he tried to figure out and found that her statement was correct. As darkness was enshrouding the earth, he changed the attire to go to Vibha with packed dinner.

Vibha was engrossed in a English novel when he entered the apartment holding the tiffin containing the eatables for dinner.

'How are you Vibha?' Pradeep enquired about her health and walked to the kitchen to serve the dinner in the plates.

He served the dinner on the table and asked Vibha to join for dinner or if she wanted he could serve over the table across the sofa as well.

On Saturday when Pradeep was opening the door of his chamber, registrar came.

'Your girl has gone?' he asked.

'Yes sir,' he told.

Placing the bag over the table he came out for the rounds of the patients. For tuesday operation list post one case of laparoscopy-diagnostic laparoscopy. She would come on Monday and I might be on leave on that day.'

Registrar noted down.

'Post the next patient of impotence, one case of cleft lip might also be posted.'

Walking they reached the ward so nurse joined them. Pradeep took hurried round of the patients. He told registrar to inspect the dressing of the labiaplasty and areolar reconstruction patient and if wounds were healed then they could be discharged.

In the evening he went to the apartment of Vibha with packed dinner. She was in the chair reclining. As Pradeep entered she sat straight. He kept the tiffin on the table across sofa. Vibha got up to serve the dinner.

'Tomorrow my father is coming to meet you,' Vibha reminded him.

'But I have told you that I shall be going to Delhi.'

'To meet Neelima,' she shrieked in anger. 'You cant go tomorrow, my father is coming and it is more important than to meet Neelima.' Her body was boiling with anger.

'Vibha, try to understand,' he tried to reason,' I have promised to Neelima.

'You will not go to Delhi,' she retorted.

Pradeep was bewildered. How could he stay back to meet her father, and for what reasons. He was not marrying her, for him glittering world of Delhi was waiting; he would go to Delhi, there herds of beauties would be lined up to marry.

'Come Pradeep dinner is served,' Vibha called him, Pradeep walked to the dining table. After dinner Pradeep was standing in drawing when Vibha retorted, 'You are not going anywhere.'

'I am going to my apartment.'

'You will stay here, will meet my father tomorrow.'

'Vibha try to understand, we should not stay together in night; if somebody had known what would happen?'

'Ok you can go if you promise me now that you will not go to Delhi tomorrow.'

'Promise,' said Pradeep to come out of melee.

Vibha came in his embrace. 'Pradeep don't break the promise. I want to get it finalized as soon as possible.'

Pradeep patted over her cheeks and assured that he was not going to Delhi following day.

Chapter 5

Pradeep got up early in the morning and hurriedly took wash to be ready by 5 so that he could reach the station by 6 in morning. He came out of apartment and started walking to the station on feet, on the way he spotted a ricksaw and called the ricksaw puller to stop and take him to railway station. On those days in city like Aligarh taxis were not available, everybody depended on ricksaws for commuting.

He paddled ricksaw to come nearer to him, Pradeep rode on the ricksaw. In the morning Vibha would come with his father and find the lock at the gate of the apartment, she would create a scene; but there was no other option. He was not interested in marrying her, but he should tell her call a spade a spade. He had to care for his career, Neelima was his future. Ricksaw was being pulled at fast pace to reach the station, at the station he paid the fare to ricksaw puller and rushed to enter the train which was about to leave the station. As soon as he entered train started moving, he took a sigh of relief. If he had been late by even one minute the train would have left the station. After settling in the train he cast his glance around to search any vacant seat; at the far end of the comprtment he spotted Maitreyi-final year MBBS student. She also saw him and immediately offered her seat to him, he walked to her and sat jostling beside her.

Maitreyi was famous student known fo her sexy features, as Pradeep jostled with her he could feel her left breast touching his arm; he enjoyed her company, caressing her breast with his forearm.

Train was running at fast pace. Neelima had promised him to receive at the station, there would be no problem.

'Where are you going sir? 'Maitreyi asked.

Pradeep turned his head more than required and looked at her boobs towering down. 'Delhi,' he told.

'You have some work over there?' She asked.

'I have to meet one of my friend,' he told then he asked, 'Do you stay in Delhi?'

'Yes sir,' she told.

'Nice,' he commented.

Train came to jeering halt at New Delhi railway station. Pradeep got out holding his luggage, jostling with others, he disembarked from the train. Maitreyi also got down and bading good bye, walked to exit.

Pradeep noticed her rounded inviting hips for the first time, he was lost in her posterior protrusions when somebody patted at her shoulders, Pradeep turned to find Neelima was standing over there.

'Hello doctor,' she stretched her hand to shake his.

Pradeep felt too awkward to shake the hand of a woman in full public view over the platform, he looked around to find if somebody was looking at them; hurriedly he shook her hand, soo soft, so smooth and silky . . .

'Oooh!' he was sensually aroused.

'Let us move, 'Neelima spelled and turned to go to exit, Pradeep following her spellbound, who was appearing even more attractive than before . . .

He was happy that he had taken the bold decision to come to Delhi and not to stay back in Aligarh and meet her father.

Neelima walked to car parked at the far end and unlocking door slid on the driver's seat, then she opened the passenger door from inside for Pradeep to enter and sit beside her. She started the car and moved, with her hand kept on steering wheel, her axillary pit could be spotted from the side, clean shaved, axilla of hers sensually aroused him and he leered further laterally to her boobs, outer edge of which was visible;

his masculinity was aroused. The silky white skin of boobs against azure blue protective cotton wrap was too sensuous.

He was completely ignited, how to tolerate the warmth of her youth. She was too warm, Pradeep thought and he would melt like wax over fire and flew all over losing his personality.

Car came to halt at red light signal in Cannaught place, when Neelima looked at Pradeep, 'Doctor how are you?'

'I am fine, and what about you?' He asked and looked at her cheeks. There were no marks of operation performed over her cheeks.

'I am fine and thankful to you, you have given me spotless face. Suddnely there was green light signal and Neelima started the car. Pradeep was looking straight apparently but leering at times at axilla and rounded edge of nubile protrusions. The azure blouse was tightly covering the boobs as if protecting them except perhaps the lateral edge. His gaze loitered from axilla to boobs and then down to silky gracious hairless glistening arm and from there to long artistic fingers. He was numb at the sight of celibate celebrity.

Car came to the jeering halt. She parked the car, got down and opened the door for Pradeep to come down, Pradeep followed her to the magnificent building through the entrance and entered into big drawing, Neelima requested him to just relax and told that she would make his arrangements for stay upstairs, he mountained up the flight of stairs and went to find the room. Pradeep was lost in her florid hips, her tightly tied azure matching saree, clinging to her wide buxom hips as if that was the azure peel of skin of Neelima.

When she went up, Pradeep cast his glance alaround.

Maid servant came holding a tray with two cups of tea. Neelima also came down, 'Take it,' she stretched her hand to give one cup to him. She lifted another cup and sat on the sofa across to him, her saree was artistically wraped over the abdomen; navel was too high and visible, it is called nabhi darshana saree, from navel down he could spot fine lanugo hair and he imagined lanugo hair merging with black silken tuft of hair enshrouding her feminine flesh and valley.

Finishing tea he kept the cup over the table and asked Neelima what had to be done.

Tidy yourelf and relax. At about 11 am we would go to meet my friend, come I shall guide you to the room, she told and walked to the stairs, Pradeep followed her. As she was ascending up the stairs he spotted writhing of knees, hips and waist underneath the azure fabric, sendng the maddening waves inside him. How would he endure the sensuality of Neelima, endure the warmth of her body . . .

Pulling his feet he followed Neelima like a pet dog, she was ascending up and he was following her . . . movements of her hips were clearly visible through fabric.

Upstairs, she turned to the left side and walked to the room he was supposed to stay, it was open, Neelima entered and Pradeep followed her.

'This is your room, relax,' said she smiling and came out swinging her hips.

Pradeep lay on the bed, legs still resting on the floor as he had not removed the shoes.

He was passing through the complicated phase. Why was she caring for him so much, did she have some ulterior motive; he had read many stories in which a beautiful lady mesmerized a male and got her work done.

Neelima was good girl, she was taking all efforts for him because he had performed operation on her. He sat on the bed and unfastened the shoestrings of shoes and became relaxed, after some time he got to his toes and took out a towel from his case and went to the bathroom to wash his face, bath room was marvelled all over, glittering in light, neat and clean, even he could see his foot prints over the floor. On the front wall of the bathroom was a window panel having mist glass which could be tilted up and down, mischieves aroused to his brain and he developed urge to glance through the window on the other side. He took a stool, ascended up and looked through the slit, on the other side which was also a bathroom; It was attached with whose room, he thought and went down; suddenly somebody entered the bathroom, Pradeep ascended again to find out who the person was, ah! she was Neelima, towel hanging from her shoulders and she was having only the skin to cover her nudity. Pradeep instead being sexually aroused felt guilty and mountained down, splashing sounds were emanating from other bathroom, Neelima was taking the bath, he again developed an urge to look at her, her nudity, her sensuous skin, her bosom, her feminine beauty, and ecstatic valley.

But supressing his urge to look at her, he decided not to peep into the other bathroom so he washed his face and came out.

Towelling the face he came out cursing the moments when he supressed his desire to look at the feminine beauty and the valley, he was a fool who had lost ooportunity to have the glimpses of nude Neelima taking the bath—Neelima the top model of India, he longed to see the jet of water splashing her boobs and the nipples, hips, waist, thighs, few drops falling over the jet black curly hair and one of the drop falling over her feminine flesh.

He could not contain himself and rushed to the bathroom to peep into the other bathroom, alack a day the bathroom was vacant.

Neelima came about half hour later, clad in back knee length skirt flanked by white shirt which was tucked beneath the skirt at waist, white glistening skin of the boobs being visible at upper border through the transparent shirt rest of the breasts were covered with black bra. It was so sensuous that he felt the rush of blood to his masculine organ and it became stiff . . .

Exuding aroma of blossoming youth, Neelima asked him to come down, Pradeep walked to ground floor, Neelima was walking in small steps as she was wearing high heel sandals over her beautiful feet, cautiously she came down.

Father and mother were sitting in the drawing on ground floor, Neelima introduced Pradeep to them. 'Mamma he is Dr Pradeep, the great Plastic surgeon from Aligarh who had performed surgery on my face.' Pradeep folded his hands to greet them.

'Neelima had talked so much about you,' mother told him.

Pradeep thanked them for kind words. 'Please take seat,' finding Pradeep standing father offered seat to him.

'No dad he will take the breakfast and then we will go for some work.' Neelima told and waved at Pradeep to the dining table. Pradeep was nervous, what her parents would have thought. They might become suscipicious of him or scold at him.

Neelima offered one chair to Pradeep and sat on other chair across the dining table.

'Neelima your parents wont say anything?' asked Pradeep.

Neelima giggled, 'What?'

'What!You are a girl and I am a man ', he stammered, Neelima was enjoying the nervousness of Pradeep.

'I mean,' Pradeep tried to say but stammered. Neelima was smiling, she kept her forearm over the dining and leaned foreward, 'We are not backward people, If you are a man, so what would you do what . . . what would you do? Perhaps nothing. It is backward thinking that a man and woman should not meet, should not live together, we don't believe in such orthodox views, which are prevalent for ages; a friend of same sex may do much more harm than the friend of the opposite sex.'

Pradeep was listening her views but more than that he was ogling at her carved out protrusions at the upper part which were inviting him to caress slowly, slowly with his tips of the fingers.

'A person of the opposite sex would not harm you but prove asset, at the most they may demand sexual favour, that's all; don't mind having sex before or after marriage. What is sex . . . just pleasure, which both gets out of physical union, what marriage is to do with it?'

Pradeep shuddered at her thoughts. God help me, he murmured to himself.

Stuffed paranthas and the pickle were served on the table by the maid, Neelima smiled to ease the building tension in Pradeep and served a parantha to him.

Pradeep took a bite, 'Delicious,' he praised.

'My maid is good at cooking,' told Neelima taking a bite at parantha, her boobs glittering in the tubelight.

'Today you are looking more beautiful,' he praised her beauty.

She giggled, 'Really!' **It is the weakness of women, they can be seduced by praising their beauty again and again, even an ugly looking girl thinks herself too attractive and can be seduced by just praise of her beauty.**

After beakfast both walked to drawing. Neelima asked Pradeep to wait for a second as she had to take out keys of the car kept in bed room.

As she walked, white sensuous legs peeping out of black skirt could be seen, he gloated his eyes rising up to reach to the upper end at silken tuft of hair. How it would feel to caress the hairy bush of her feminine grove.

Shifting his gaze to her posterior protrusions he found that saree was better dress to show the beauty of posterior protrusions, saree if tied properly exhibit nothing but shows everything writhing of every inch of ones' sensuous posteriors.

'How was the breakfast?' Mother walked to Pradeep and asked.

'It was nice,' he answered plainly.

'You have performed an excellent operation at my daughter's face,' mother congratulated him.

'Thank you,' Pradeep thanked for nice words.

'She is very innocent girl now 25 years, yet not interested in marriage we don't know how to persuade her; a girl should have been married by this age she has attained, society start asking dfferent set of questions I was married at the age of 16 years.'

'I do agree,' Pradeep agreed.

Neelima came swinging the key ring in her index finger.

'Come,' she called Pradeep walking out to the car. She enterd the driver's seat unlocking the car and opened the door on other side for Pradeep to enter. Starting the car she came on the main road.

Suddenly she had to apply brakes as a scooter hailing from the wrong side took sharper turn, Pradeep looked at her shapely legs which applied brakes while she was abusing the scooter driver in Enlglish.

Pradeep smiled timidly. Suddenly car turned to the left and Pradeep jostled with her, his head resting against her protrusions over the bosom; he straightned soon.

'Sorry,' he spelled, Neelima opened her lips a bit, smiled exotically but did not spell the words.

Car came to halt in front of Grover's nursing home, switching off the engine, Neelima got down from the car and slammed the door. Pradeep disembarked from other side and followed her mountaining up stairs leading to reception area, as she was ascending up one of her thighs was visible which aroused Pradeep fiercely.

'Is Dr Grover Inside?' Neelima enquired to receptionist.

'Yes madam he is inside waiting for you.'

Neelima entered the chamber of Dr Grover and shook his hands, Pradeep also entered rallying behind Neelima.

'Meet my friend Pradeep,' she introduced Pradeep to Dr Grover. 'Glad to meet you,' Grover shook his hand and offered a seat.

He sat down.

'She said that you wanted to settle your practice of plastic surgery in Delhi good idea, come once a week initially, later on depending on the number of the patients frequency of the visits could be increased.'

'Yes I agree, 'Pradeep agreed.

'Since when do you want to start.'

Before Padeep could say anything, Neelima said,' From today.' Then she turned to Pradeep and said, 'I would be your first patient, examine me and tell me what more could be done to make me prettier,' she giggled.

Receptionist called Grover over phone and told that a patient wanted to consult about mammoplasty.

'Send her in,' Grover asked the receptionist to send the patient inside, and then turned to Pradeep,' You are lucky, a patient has come for mammoplasty, I have never got any enquiry for mammoplasty in last two years as no plastic surgeon is attached with this nursing home; you have entered and the patient had come,' Grover told.

Pradeep smiled meekly and Neelima giggled.

Patient came inside. She told that she wanted to undergo mammoplasty.

Grover introduced Dr Pradeep to the patient, an young girl in her early teens. 'Dr Pradeep is eminent plastic surgeon of India.'

'Pradeep sir tell me some details,' she asked.

'For mammoplasty silicone implants are placed inside the breasts which give instant enlargement. I will like to examine and tell you further details.'

Grover called the nurse and told her that Dr Pradeep would examine madam, 'he waved his finger towards the patient,' Help him in carrying out the examination.'

'Ok sir,' nurse bowed down her head and went out with patient and Pradeep. In the examination room, Pradeep asked nurse to request the patient to bare her bosom so that she could be examined. The patient hesitated initially but soon she pulled her shirt up for Pradeep to examine. Her breasts were smaller having bra size of 28 only Pradeep found on examination.

'How much increase in size do you want?' Pradeep asked.

'May be 36, is that possible doctor?' She asked.

'Yes.'

After examining her Pradeep walked to the chamber where Neelima was talking to Grover, stooping forward over the table so that her rounded protuberances were peeping out of her white shirt. The milky white skin of her bosom was gleaming. Pradeep was envious of Grover Neelima should not have been so closer to him. When Neelima found Pradeep standing over there she asked, 'What have you examined? Breasts, right? What is the size?'

Pradeep did not like her questions, though he had become passionate at the sight of girls but not the patients; the relation between patients and doctor is pious and it should be regarded. Neelima was different she was his girl friend and not the patient, he settled in the chair.

'Doctors are lucky. People come to see what others are keen to see even by offering money,' she commented and giggled, they spend the money for glimpses. What is cabaret, glimpses of feminine beauty and doctors see the full view, unhindered and take money for seeing them bare.

Pradeep was not convinced, 'I don't agree with you, when docor see a patient, he or she is a patient and not feminine beauty.'

Dr Grover agreed with Pradeep, patient is patient male or female does not matter much for the doctor.

Neelima smiled seductively. 'Grover don't talk like this, I know many of the doctors who take advnatage of female patients.'

'They must be exceptions, one fish makes the whole pond wrought.'

The patient entered the chamber.

'You breasts can be enlarged, for which silicon implants are to be placed inside boobs,' Pradeep told the patient who had just entered.

'Is there any risk, in future deliveries, or pregnancies?'

'No.'

'Ok, doctor, I will contact you soon,' said she and getting to her toes walked away. 'So you start from next Sunday, we will book the patients,' Grover told.

'Ok,' Neelima said and shook his hand, got to her toes, and came to the car. In the car Neelima said, 'Pradeep you would be famous soon, herds of girls would flock to you to enhance beauty of their bodies,' she gigged. 'I would introduce you to many of my friends—males and females alike.' She cluctched his hand, 'I have many female friends who will be after you to get themselves studded with big boobs. Car was racing at Shahjahan road from where Neelima turned car to Pandara road for lunch.

Neelima was complicated women, he thought. She was quite different than what he thought, the way she commented about patients and the doctors' fortune was not reasonable. She should have respected doctors and have regard for patient doctor relationship. Her brain always thought of sex. He was too impressed with her at Aligarh by her behaviour, but in Delhi her behaviour was quite different. Her saree was not properly fastened he had seen her posterior protrusions, he thought and casted a glance at her protrusions, his hand was stroking her palm slowly and slowly with finger tip of index and then he started to move the finger tip slowly over the skin of palm, mere touch of which was so sensuous that his body had innumerable waves going allover his body and his masculine flesh was becoming stiff with extra rush of the blood. Neelima was feeling the touch of his finger tip, masculine brown skin against her glistening white skin was making her fluid ready to flow alaround him and to be one with him. The fluid was there, she had felt, inside her feminine valley as well, wetting the guarding fleshes of her secret valley, and exiting out to her protective covering. She longed for him to ford in the river of passion inside her valley, fiercely to engulf all fluid and then exude more fluid and let there be fluids alaround.

After lunch they returned home when Pradeep expressed his desire to go back to Aligarh.

'Doctor you cant go today, have to stay tonight. Go tomorrow morning,' requested Neelima clutching his hand and almost pulling him up to the stairs.

Pradeep did not resist and mountained up with Neelima. She told him to relax, in the evening they would go to boat club at India gate.

Pradeep was also in no mood to go, he should stay tonight, might be he got a chance to see Neelima taking the bath in all her nudity, and his masculine flesh hardened at the mere thought of seeing her naked flesh, her primitive instincts woke up and he had intense desire to guide the hardened flesh inside her feminine exotic cavern, slowly initially and then make her dance like in congo, she following him as leader to reach at the peak of ecstacy and suddenly for dance to stop when there is clappings allover her body, which would have writhed in orgasm, sexy and mind blogging orgasm . . .

He walked to his room when the phone bell rang. Call was from Vibha, unsure, he rejected the call, but she persisted, forcing Pradeep to take her call.

'What happened to you man, you are rejecting my calls,' she retorted.

He was nervous, could not make up his mind what to say. 'Are you listening,' she was fierce.

'Yes Vibha, how are you?'

'I am going to hell,' she squeaked. 'What about the promise you made, and you went to Delhi, now listen, father has come I have persuaded him to stay overnight; come in the night to my apartment to discuss about marriage affairs,' she told him sternly.

'My God,' his masculine strong flesh had become limp. 'Vibha . . . I am not sure . . .'

'Sure!What do you mean? You have to come in the evening, and today,' she screamed as loudly as possible.

If she comes to know I am staying back with Neelima, she would tear me in pieces. Oh Pradeep!. Only God can save you . . .

He came to life when Vibha's nightmare was over. He had got one patient of mammoplasty, he would perform tomorrow. He was amazed at behaviour of Neelima so open, so uninhibited—and dress, in the morning she was wearing so low saree even the silky tuft of her feminine hair could be seen the feminine charm is to be shown to your own man and not to everybody, and then her shirt which was exhibiting upper half of the boobs, shamelessly; her comments about the patient and doctor relations were also not upto the mark. Doctors are not in flesh trade to caress the boobs and enjoy the patients'bodies. Patients come for releief of sufferings and not the enjoyment . . . Head started aching so he thumped his forehead with the heel of the palm and after sometime sprang to his toes, pulled out a towel and enterd the bathroom. Towelling his face he returned to the room, put on loose trouser and shirt and lay on the bed. No sooner than he lay on the bed, he slept.

When he awoke, it was four in the evening, he sat on the bed and came to his toes to come out of the room, peered out of verandah there was huge park below having lush greenery; he threw his glance all around and then at the room Neelima was inside, the door of the room was closed. He developed same primitive instinct, to run and caress her, to get his hardenes inside her, fiercely so that she reached at the peak of cliff with ferocity so that she begged for more and more enjoyment . . . .

When he entered the room, splashes were emnating from the other bathroom. Was Neelima taking bath he imagined and immediately lifted the stool to keep just below the window to peep into adjacent bath room. Neelima was there, but he could get the glimpse of her hands and feet only as she was lying in bathtub and his most part of bare body was not visible.

He was mad with passion and forced his face in the slit between the glass and window to get glimpses of naked flesh of Neelima and suddenly a nail pierced his forehead.

'Oohhhh!' he screamed, but cutting the scream with his teeth, he got down, as a defeated player and sat on the bed. Sometimes his behaviour was irrational, he was interested in having glimpses of her bare body, had he not seen naked females before, it is immoral and not expected of a doctor of his repute . . . . he was thinking.

Chapter 6

Neelima knocked at the door and walked into the room. She was aghast finding blood streakes on the floor. 'Where the blood has come from? What happened?' She asked Pradeep.

How should he tell that he was trying to glance at her naked body, he thought.

'What had happened?' She asked again and sat beside him on the bed.

'Just slipped,' he told stammering.

'In bathroom?'

'Yes,' said Pradeep hurriedly and became anxious because if she went to bathroom he would have no explanation for the stool lying in the bathroom.

He suddenly sprang up on his toes, Neelima prevented him from getting down and told that she was bringing the dressing set, he should stay on bed. Pradeep sat on the bed.

When Neelima went out of the room Pradeep got to his toes hurriedly and rushed to the bathroom to bring the stool out from there. At the same time Neelima returned with dressing set, 'Why have you got up, lie down over the bed, I shall dress it.' Pradeep followed her like a child and lay on the bed. She cleaned the area with spirit, Pradeep cried in agony, got hold the hand of Neelima. Neelima rebuked him, 'You are patient at present, lie down.'

After the dressing the wound she got up and told Pradeep that he should rest, she would bring tea for him.

Neelima was very caring though she had put on the dress which was revealing her body and he did not like, but he should not forget that Delhi was advanced city, she had to wear such revealing dresses; he was too narrow minded.

Neelima entered holding tray having two cups of tea and some biscuits. She put the tray on table and lifting the cup stretched her hand to give to Pradeep. She was wearing pink frock, Pradeep sighted short frock through which he could see the two shapely thighs emanating and his glance ascended up where he wanted to get glimpse of her feminine beauty, but view was obstructed by the protective covering of the frock. Was she wearing the protective covering for coverage of most intimate feminine flesh also.

Mother of Neelima also rallied behind her. 'How are you? How did it happen?' She asked.

'Just by the way I skidded, nothing serious mom, 'told Pradeep and felt ashamed of himself when he rememberd how did it happen. If she had known that he was trying to get the glimpses of the naked body of her daughter she would turn him away from the house.

'Ok take care,' she said and went out.

'Your mother is nice,' commented Pradeep when she went away.

Neelima smiled. 'We are broadminded and do not believe in backward thinking, believe that sex and marriage are two separate issues and should not be clubbed together, marriage is a pious bond and it should not be abused by clubbing sex to it.'

She was speaking Pradeep looking at her unable to understand, too complicated, approved pre and extramarital sex; how he would approve that at all, sex was pious and sensuous union of two lovers and that should not be made out of bond of marriage. Leaving aside her thinking for sex she was good natured girl.

'Like to go to boat club still?' She asked taking a gulp of coffee.

'Nothing had happened to me, we would go to boat club,' Pradeep told.

'If you are not feeling alright, we should postpone it for some other day,' she suggested.

'Its minor cut, doesn't matter, we will go,' he said and got to his toes. 'I am putting on the dress, and just in ten minutes would be ready to go.'

'Ok,' Neelima agreed and walked out of the room.

Her thighs are superb, glistening skin, would automatically lead to ecstatic place of feminine beauty, if a finger is put. In the afternoon in the car she had put the hand over his hand, he should have caressed her hand and put a kiss on her lips but he could not do it.

Pradeep was very simple doctor, Neelima thought while in her room, when she put her hand over his, he remained unmoved. He should have caressed her hand and did something further, like should have caressed thighs or kissed at lips. She would make him to do all such nasty things, must be afeared of . . . . 'Swainish boy,' she yelled and giggled.

She returned after sometime in the same dress and called Pradeep to come out of the room, he came out and followed her downstairs. In the frock her posteriors were not ecstatically visible as were in tight saree in the morning, which was too sensuous; why her frock was so loose, it could be tighter at posteriors.

Double standard of morality, when she was bearing tight saree he enjoyed her sensous hips but when others ogled at her he thought that immodest, and when she was wearing frock which was little loose at poseriors, he was cursing her for not having tighter dress over the posteriors; **men always want to enjoy the nudity of women but talks of morality so that others don't enjoy of such glimpses.**

Neelima parked the car at boat club and got down Pradeep climbing down from other side and joining Neelima in going to ticket window to purchase tickets for boating. Neelima opted for one hour ride and paid the money. Holding the tickets she walked to parking bay for the boats where she handed over the tickets to incharge who waved them to descend down in one of the boat. Neelima followed him and climbed down in the boat followed by Pradeep who while climbing down skidded and to avoid fall he took support of Neelima when his hand cupped soft swell on her bosom, immediately he straightened himself and said, 'Sorry.' Neelima smiled.

Mere touch of swell of her bosom caused rush of blood throughout his body which started throbbing. Neelima sat on the driver's seat and started paddling the boat, Pradeep joined her in paddling.

'Neelima you have to paddle my boat also, I am too swainish don't know how to start; you have to start and paddle the boat of the life,' he suggested.

'I will paddle your boat also Dr Pradeep, you are swainish doctor, dont know how to proceed; in the afternoon I expected you to kiss me, If some of the other friend might have been present, in this dress he would have removd frock first and then ravished me fiercely, deeply, and took me to the crest of sexual pleasure. But you behaved as impotent person, don't worry I will make you perfect in the matter of sex.'

'I love boating', Neelima told. 'Almost every Sunday I come over here.'

'With whom?' He asked.

'Not a definite partner, sometimes with Ruchika and other male friends also,' she giggled. Boat had reached at the other end, when they stopped paddling, Neelima rested her head against his shoulder. Pradeep I will teach the chapter of sex. She said to herself and grinned.

Weather was pleasant, clouds were overflowing sky as if to enshroud two lovers with a cotton wrap or enshroud the beautiful boobs of a gorgeous woman by protective wrap. Neelima raised her head and sat reclining, looked into his eyes when masculine energy crept through her body making her fluid and she slid her lips over his to give a sensuous kiss. I have to do it Pradeep, actually you should have initiated, but you are too moron. Kiss made pradeep passionate, his body tingling and blood rushing to his organs making it to throb. She felt the hardness male hardness against her thighs and in a fit encircled his neck with her arm showering kisses as if in hurry to kiss him over his lips, cheeks and forehead . . .

At dinner mother of Neelima asked, 'Son which place do you belong?'

'Agra.'

'Your parents are staying over there?'

'Yes.'

'Neelima talked so much about you all praise for you, she is our only child, both of us love her too much never go against her wishes but,' she stammered, 'She is still celibate.'

'Oh mamma,' Neelima interrupted.

'Keep silent,' she quipped,' I am talking to my son.'

Pradeep was enjoying verbal duet, he also quipped,' Yes mamma is talking to me, why are you interfering?'

'Cheat,' Neelima pressed his right foot with her sandal fiercely. Pradeep winced. Mother observed him wincing so she asked,' What happened? Some pain?'

'Mamma he is having pain in tummy, at boat club also he was telling that he was having pain,' Neelima told mother as she wanted to teach a lesson to Pradeep.

'Then don't eat any thing, I will bring milk for you,' mother suggested.

'Yes don't eat, mamma will bring milk for you,' Neelima giggled subduedly. Loudly she said, 'Rest upstairs, I shall bring milk for you.'

Pradeep looked at her frowning, now he had to starve and take milk only.

'My son, go and rest upstairs, she shall bring milk for you,' mother persisted.

Pradeep got up cursing Neelima, as he strolled Neelima giggled again subduedly spearing Pradeep into two.

He lied on the bed cursing Neelima, after some times she came with a glass of milk. He closed his eyes and pretended as if he was sleeping. She kept the glass over the table and sat beside him on the bed.

'Pradeep,' she called on him.

He did not open eyes.

'I know that you are not asleep,' she commented, 'I am sorry Pradeep.'

He gave a reedy smile and sat on the bed, Neelima rested her head agansint his chest. 'I am sorry,' she yelled again.

'What was need of making a story that he was having pain?'

'I am so sorry Pradeep,' she yelled and put her head against his chest.

'Its alright,' Pradeep said and put his fingers in her hair stroking it.

'Take milk,' she offered jerking hair back and stretched her arm to give the glass of milk to him.

Pradeep got hold of the glass and smiled, 'You are too naughty.'

She giggled looking at him pouring the milk inside stomach. After finishing milk he kept the glass over the stool kept adjacent to bed. Neelima got to her toes,' I shall come back within few minutes,' she said and walked out of the room.

Pradeep lay on the bed after taking milk. Had mother thought of marrying Neelima to him, it might be because she had been so soft with him mothers of grown up girls speak nicely to an accompanying boys only if they liked the boys and wished to marry their daughters to them.

After some times Neelima came back. She called him out side, 'Come, Pradeep come out side in verandah. Pradeep got up to his feet and putting his feet in sandals came out of room, Neelima clutched his hand and walked to the extreme end of verandah. She was in green nighty through which her swell on bosom were visible and so were her thighs. Pradeep glanced at her bosom . . .

'How are you feeling now?' Neelima asked while she sat on parapet. He frowned upon her comment but did not yell a word.

Glances through her boobs were maddening he put his hand over her protuberance, Neelima got hold of his hand and removed. 'Sorry Neelima, I am so sorry,' said Pradeep. 'I should not have misbehaved with you. Putting the hand over breasts of a woman is outraging her modesty. I should not have done,' he said.

'Pradeep you are really moron. My boobs are throbbing should be be solaced by the cup of your hand, cup my boobs Pradeep, cup them, go down and caress my tuft of hair, and further deep, put my burning cave to ease by your soothing man, by soothing but stiff masculine organ, oh Pradeep do something.' Neelima was thinking but did not say presently.

Pradeep again said, 'I am sorry Neelima.'

Neelima did not utter a word what to say to this moron doctor, how to teach him the chaper of love, she never thought doctors were so moron in matters of love and sex.

She was beholding at full moon. 'It is too dull in font of you,' Pradeep commented.

'Really so!' Neelima appreciated the comment and put her arms around him, putting her lips over his as if trying to explore something, somewhere, if not over the lips then inside, beneath the tongue or somewhere there, 'Pradeep I love you,' Her body was tensed, hot as if embered by fierce flow of sexual energy in her body.

The flow of blood inside her body was at very fast pace, whole body was throbbing pulsating and writhing for his manly stiffness but he was sitting idle, not moving any structure hand lips or any thing else. Neelima had been disgruntled with Pradeep. How to teach him lessons of love, moron doctor, had just commented, it is dull infront of you, huh, what to do . . . ?

Suddenly she got up and ran back to her room. Pradeep took notice of that but kept on sitting for long hours over there expecting she would return, when she did not return he walked to her room. She was in her room lying on the bed her body throbbing due to intensified flow of blood.

'Neelima are you angry?' He asked entering the room. She jumped, sprang to her feet and caught hold of him her arms around him.

Heat emanating from prodding peaks of her bosom maddened him passionately and he felt his masculinity stiffening, she also felt the hardness but again the same story, he was not doing any thing not even kissing. Frustrated she took the lead and put her lips over his to which he responded by kissing over her lips, slowlely descending down over her neck . . . holding her with his arm, he pushed his hand beneath the protective covering of the night dress, caressed her pulsating swells over bosom . . .

'Ah!' she purred in passion. 'Pradeep I love you, long for and wish to be ravished by you,' she said in husky voice.

'Neelima I too love you,' he said in sexually charged voice his hand cupping the swells over the bosom which had become taut by extra rush of blood and the ecstatic peak had become stiff like cliff. He took the stiff cliff in between thumb and forefinger and caressed slowely to make it harder. Slowly he disrobed her of protective cotton wrap over the bosom and the ecstatic swells were bare prodding foreward in arrogance with pink small stiff flesh prodding forward still further. Mad in passion, he cupped the both evections and caressed both stiff fleshy knobs.

Neelima was reaching at peak of orgasm and wanted him to insert his hugely stiff manly organ in side her cave and take her to the peak of ecstasy, she unrobed herself as if in hurry to get the act completed and got hold of his huge organ after pulling down the trousers; and he was about to become one in union, when he suddenly jerked and moved from Neelima. It is immoral and he should not do it. Neelima was awestruck and in attack of frenzy she pushed Pradeep away,' You are impotent, bloody doctor you have to be taught the manners of love and sex. Go away at present go away . . . . run . . .

Chapter 7

Neelima got up early in the morning as she had to drop Pradeep at railway station, train was scheduled to leave at 7 am.

She knockd at the door, Pradeep was already awoke so he opened the door. 'Good morning Neelima,' he welcomed her and closed the door on her back. 'Oh! you are ready,' Neelima said.

'Yes, I am,' Pradeep spelled, nothing reminicient on his face of previous evening.

Neelima looked at his face. He was a man who did not perform the act, did not quench her thirst, and there was no sign of sorrow over his face what type of doctor he had been. The whole night she was lost in finding the answer for his irrational behaviour. Was he homo, as one of her friend was telling that her husband was homo and never took interest in physical relations with her, otherwise being normal male. Was that the case with Dr Pradeep too? A big dark spot appeared before her eyes and suddenly smoke started bellowing up and slowly whole of the room became filled with smoke. She got up and rushed outside feeling suffocated. The moon was in full youth, same moon which was told to be duller in front of her . . . If he had been homo, how could he feel those emotions and feelings about her . . . he could not be homo, she was sure . . . Then? And again a big dark spot appeared before her, fearing suffocated again she ran down . . .

'Neelima where are you lost?' Asked Pradeep. She came to life, 'Nothing. Alright, I am going down and serving breakfast if you are ready then come down,' she said and started to go down, wearing black jeans flanked by pink top, she was appearing superb.

Neelima served the breakfast over the dining table and waved Pradeep to come over to the table.

Pradeep got to his toes and walked to the table to sit across Neelima, lifted the cup and took a sip. 'Its tasty tea, have you prepared?'

'Yes.' Neelima said plainly. The lines of torture were visible over her face, torture of feminism by masculinity, torture of being burnt while loads of water could have been sprinkled to save her torture of feeling the painful throbbings inside her when it could have been silenced by rapid flow of masculine fluid. But nothing of that kind took place and she kept on writhing the whole night, the signs of which were visible on her face in the form of puffy face and swollen red eyes.

'Are you sick?'

Sick. yes she was sick, sick of him sick of her behaviour and sick of his masculine warmth which could have made her purring allover, but she had been made sick, these moron men do not understand what women need, what women desire, when they desire, it has to be fulfilled, if not fulfilled, their body reponds very badly. Her body had become awestricken, diseased as if the while nectar from her flower had been thrown away, not sucked . . . if it couldhave been sucked, she would have become a glowing beauty in the morning. Oh moron doctor, you would kill me . . .

'I could not sleep the whole night.'

'Why?'

Even after tormenting her he was asking why she had not been able to sleep. Funny man, irrational, what to answer . . . she remained silent.

'Are you annoyed with my misbehaviour?'

'Misbehaviour! When have you misbehaved with me?' Neelima frowned upon.

'I should not have done it.'

'What?' she squeaked.

'I caressed your boobs, and . . . ,' he mumbled.

'Pradeep you are too innocent and simple, you have caressed the boobs of whom, your girl friend, of a girl who is in love with you; it is of no singnificance, leave it. I wont have mind having sex with you, won't mind having pre or extra marital sex. We are quite forward and don't mind fondling, and snogging. They are as simple as shaking the hands,' she pacified him putting the empty cup of tea over the table. 'Finish your breakfast, I am taking out the car from garage,' she told him and got to her toes took out the keys of car and walked to the gate.

Pradeep was baffled, took a sip of tea, 'For her fondling of boobs was like shaking the hands, Pradeep be careful, the girl was too fast for him, forget her . . .'

'He had been too innocent, what to do with him, yesterday he just frustrated her, she was sexually excited, and poor fellow ran away talking of morality. My God, I should have slapped on him. How she would be comfortable with him, she would make him extrovert,' she thought and opening the door of car sat on driver seat. Pradeep had also come with luggage and sat beside her on passenger seat.

'So you will come the next Sunday,' she asked.

'Yes.'

'In that case just give me a call, I will pick you up from the station,' she said and starting the car came on the road to railway station. Driving the car at low speed she said, 'Pradeep why did you behave in the way you should not have yesternight?'

'I am so sorry.'

'Pradeep you need not be sorry, but I still owe an answer from you. When molten fluid is over flowing all over how and why it should be stopped. It had to be silenced, cooled down and I could not undertand how would you be able to control when I could not myself and kept on burning the whole night.' she said and looked at him who was sitting silently. Suddenly a cycle puller took a left turn and she had to press sudden breaks, She abused the cyclepuller which perhaps he could not listen as the doors of car and glasses of windows were closed.

She stopped the car in front of railway station. It was 6. 30 and there was about 30 minutes for train to leave. Occupying the seat in the compartment Pradeep came out, Neelima was waiting, 'Do phone me when you reach.'

'Yes,' Pradeep looked at her in pink shirt was too ecstatic and through that her boobs were prodding out. He should not think of her so much, her thinking about sex and life were too advanced to be endured by him. Train started moving so Pradeep shook her hand and entrained when he spotted Maitreyi who was running on the platform to board the train. As she tried to enter the train, her foot slipped and she was about to fall when Pradeep swopped down over her grabbed and pull her inside. She was resting against Pradeep who was holding her for little more time than required. Maitreyi herself was not longing to part away. She was panting for breath. 'Sir thank you very much, you have saved me from fall. Thank you.'

'Maitreyi, are you mad? I must have moved to act and save for that matter any other girl also,' and he mumbled, 'I mean anybody.'

Her boobs were rising and falling with every breath Pradeep was enjoying the writhing of her boobs against his chest.

She parted away after sometimes as she had to part away. Pradeep carefully examined her for any injury, as there was none he supported her in walking and took to a vacant seat where his belongings were kept. Maitreyi sat down with a thud, still dazed with eyes wide open. What would had happened had she fell down, her arm might have been amputated or the leg or might be the face, she shuddered. Pradeep felt the quivering of her body and he put his hand around his neck, 'Be calm, now you are safe,' Pradeep assured her he was in no mood to remove the arm as its inner part was by the side of florid carvings through which the feminine energy was insinuating inside his body and he was feeling sudden rush of blood to make the few of his organs turgid.

'Sir, I am so thankful to you, you really saved me,' she rested her head against his shoulder. He raked his finger in hairlorn, 'Cool down Maitreyi,' he said.

Vibha must kill him, she must be like a rabid animal. He should not have behaved with her like this, her father had come, he should have returned to Aligarh in the evening. But Neelima had seduced him, he was in no mood to go back to Aligarh yesterday. Vibha would be furious. He would marry a beautiul girl like Neelima, but her behaviour had forced him to change the mind. And he was in dilemma—Vibha or Neelima.

The girl sitting next to him was also good option, he thought, beautiful like Neelima and simple like Vibha, she might be a good choice. He turned his neck to look down upon her who by then had slept head resting against his shoulder and upper part of boobs visible, quite a bit which again caused the rush of the blood to his whole body stiffening the masculinity.

After some time she woke up to find herself against Pradeep, boobs almost becoming naked and he being pressed with fresh rush of blood at frequent intervals leading to frequent stiffenings. 'I am so sorry,' she got up and started arranging hair which had splayed alaround.

Train stopped at Aligarh railway station, so Pradeep got up and suppoted her also in getting up. 'I am alright sir.'

Pradeep did not pay any attention to her words and holding his case came out supporting her also. Out side he took her to the ricksaw helped her to ascend on that Pradeep mountaining up from other side. Ricksaw puller started pulling the ricksaw.

Maitreyi was by his side when he shifted the position his fingers touched hers and he clutched the fingers softly and kept on holding for longer time. Maitreyi smiled and slowly sniggled out of the Pradeep. From Dodpur ricksaw turned to left to go to SN hall—a hostel for ladies. 'Sir I would go,' she protested.

'Don't try to be brave,' he rebuked her though he rebuked her he wanted to be with her for longer time as clutching her fingers touch of fingers had again flown the blood to his sensous organs. Passing through the jungle he encircled her neck and put his lips over hers. Maiteryi was taken aback, but she liked it and praised to be like that for ever. Dropping her at SN hall he returned to the medical college, when he felt vaccum, vaccum in life as some thing had been lost as if his life had been dropped behind as if he had become lifeless. What was happening to him, he had become mad in love, love with whom, love with maitreyi?

In the medical college he went straight to OPD, registrar was examining the patients. As he saw Pradeep, he got up and wished good morning, 'How are the patients?' Pradeep asked.

'All of the patients are alright, I have taken the round.'

'And how many beds are vacant?'

'One in female ward and one in male ward, after admission of the patient you had told me to admit for laparoscopy.'

After OPD Pradeep went to the ward for taking the round of the patients, he had admitted two more patients from OPD. In the male ward the patient was admitted for management of cancer of the cheek and in the female ward for abdominoplasty. In the female ward Pradeep asked registrar to shift the patient to dressing room. 'Which patient?' he asked.

'Abdominoplasty patient.'

Registrar went and shifted the patient to the dressing room, Pradeep inspected the dressing and walked back to his chamber, he searched for the book of microsurgery of the tubes from the book shelf when Vibha entered. She was in bad mood and caught hold his collar, 'Mr Pradeep, you are too mean. I have never seen a wolff, a rascal like you . . . I always took you a gentle doctor, but yesterday I came to know that you are too mean, playing with my emotions. You are too mean and I am too foolish to let you play with my emotions. You are rascal and sex starved, just as any other man is. All the men are alike, sex starved, loitering behind beautiful females like their pet dogs. Huh . . . too mean she chided abused and looked at him indignantly.

Pradeep was nervous and too disconcerted, 'Try to understand, Vibha. It was essential for me to go to Delhi.' He got collar relased from her clutches. If somebody else had entered, what would happenen.

'What about your promise of not going to Delhi,' she squeaked in full voice.

'Vibha at that time you had been too emotional so I made the promise.'

'So you don't bother for my emotions?'

'I dont mean that,' Pradeep stammered.

'And why did you not come back in the night?'

He had no words, what to say. He was in remorse. 'I am sorry.'

'I had been knowing that you dont love me, but I had not known that you were too mean and I was made fool of your love,' she thrusted him and walked out of the chamber.

He had done wrong to her, Pradeep thought. At least in the evening he should have returned, particularly when there was not much to do in Delhi. But Neelima was there, and he was longing to see her naked body, too mean, Vibha was right. He saw himself indignantly and found tide of waves as if in ocean and he was drowned . . . save me . . . save me . . . he cried . . . .

Neelima was Neelima, her evections on the bosom immediately aroused him, he wanted to see them nake and her nipples, ah! Pradeep again felt rush of blood to his genitals felt some stiffness, as he came out of tide of waves he thought. It is true for men world over, **body of women is great fascination for them.**

Vibha was in anger but that became fluid within no time, after she manhandled Pradeep. She had never done so before, but that day she was in very bad mood, she had called father for fixing some date and he had gone to Delhi. Anyway he could persuade her father to stay back, told him that Pradeep would be coming back from home, where he had gone because of some emergency problems. Whatever it was, he was his man and she could not afford to lose him to her, the witch, the wench woman, Neelima, who would defeat her, and she was not easy to accept the defeat.'

Pradeep was in remorse, what to do how to cajole Vibha, her mood was really bad. However he had to decide what did he want. Neelima was difficult girl and he would not be able to tolerate her, she was too hot to handle, his whole body would be charred in her company and Vibha, she was bent upon marrying but he was not interested to marry her.

After taking round of the patients Vibha was in the chamber in bad mood, she had persuaded her father to stay back, how to ask Pradeep to go and meet him. Let us forget everything, he had misbehaved with her and she had misbehaved with him. But he was her man, Pradeep, her love.

She got up and decided to go to Pradeeep and sort out the differences with him. She came back and entered the chamber of Pradeep who became nervous finding her again in the chamber, but she was fluid this time. 'Pradeep I am sorry, you should have understood my situation, father had wanted to meet you, I could persuade him to stay back.' She got hold of him and requested, 'Please come for lunch at my apartment, please.'

Pradeep just nodded and pulling her hand gave a sensuous kiss, which made her smile, 'You are too naughty, I shall make you plain after marriage, Neeelima had spoilt you, the wench and witch. Now you would not go Delhi.'

'Come, I shall wait for you to lunch,' she said and walked out of the room. Pradeep was in better mood, as Vibha was ok, he did not want to annoy her. She was his classfellow and his friend as well, friend who really cared for him. However he should not keep her in dark, should tell her that he would marry Neelima, let him take lunch and meet her father, but afterwards he would tell Vibha that he wanted to marry Neelima.

However Neelima was haunting him, she had said she did not mind having pre or extramarital sex, which meant she must be having sexual relations with others and after marriage she would have sex with others, mere thought of her ecstatic valley which would not be unbanned for the first time for him on the honeymoon night, that valley was not unblemished made him disconcerted . . .

But in no time he was again lost in her boobs, he should have explored her boobs, her boobs and her feminine beauty. He was a fool to run away when there had been an opportunity to explore the ecstatic feminine valley and become fluid over there, fluid all over wetting feminism, but he ran away from scene.

At two he came to his apartment for lunch, whether to go to Vibha's apartment or not, he could go for lunch, but he would not marry her would marry Neelima; he walked to the window and peered out at medico girls going to the hostel, chuckling and giggling, and amongst them spotted, she was also having big and carved out swells visible through protective cotton wrap.

He turned to walk inside and sat on the sofa, what to do? Should he go to her apartment or not. There was no objection to meet her father, If he decided not to meet then she would create havoc he did not want to lose her either.

At three he came out of his apartment and went to Vibha's. She was waiting for him. 'Papa, he is Pradeep,' she introduced Pradeep to her father.

Father was too courteous he spang to his feet and shook his hand, 'Vibha had talked so much of you that I feel pleased to meet you see you in person, come have a seat,' he offered the seat to him.

Pradeep was impressed with his manners, opposite to what Vibha used to say, very strict and bla bla . . .

Vibha brought water for Pradeep, 'Papa will you take water?' She asked.

Her father denied as he had taken water few minutes back.

Pradeep took the glass of water and sat straight to drink it.

'Vibha is much impressed by you what is your opinion about her? If you think it suitable I shall like to meet your father to talk about marriage. She is growing old, and sooner it is solemnized better it is.'

Pradeep said, 'Yes papa I also think so.' He kept the glass on the table. Vibha bent down to lift the glass when Pradeep hold the glass to give that to Vibha, and at that time the fingers of both interwined. Pradeep got hold of her hand for a longer time, when she bit her lowe lip and got her hand released. In front of father he was behaving as if he loved her so much.

Vibha was exulting. Even if he had gone to Delhi, he was her man and now on wards she wont allow him to go to Delhi. Neelima was really a witch, who could mesmerize my man with her charm. It was not his fault but her folly.

Pradeep after lunch came out of her apartment, meeting had ended on succesful note, Pradeep promised to convince his father to meet at some mutually agreed place. So he was not relaxed, he had promised all that just to please Vibha she had been her friend for 15 years; he was sure to marry to her also, but intrusion of Neelima had thwarted all plans when he had become double minded and not in mood to marry to Vibha.

Neelima was stunning beauty indeed, stunning boobs stunning thighs stunning posteriors; every thing stunning. On railway station when she came to drop him, her shot shirt was high and waist of jeans was portraying her pink panties through which bare flesh of her posteriors has caused the rush of blood in his limp flesh. In last 24 hours he had been aroused so many times in the yester evening he was about to insert her stony hard man in the ecstatic valley to become fluid but he ran away from the scene. He should not have done, she was too fluid ready to make him fluid with warmth of her feminine charm but he ran away. She might think him impotent otherwise why a normal man would run away when the whole beauty of sprawling lawn was lying naked in front of him, could caress the tuft of green grass and also the feminine flesh, longing to be stimulated to take her to the ectstatic peak of physical pleasure.

The only point against was her cloudy character, the sprawling lawn should be for him only and not for others to take a stroll, and if that is not assured, he would not marry her.

He would not give birth to another Mrs Maheshwari, who would run amuck for sex. He would not be able to tolerate his wife going to anther man for dalliance.

Walking he reached to his apartment, when he took out the mobile phone from his trouser and called Neelima, she had asked to call her. She picked up the phone.

'Pradeep how are you?' She enquired. 'Reached safely.'

'I am fine, reached in morning and then went to hospital.'

'Pradeep I miss you a lot, You have mesmerized me by your charm, too simple, could not sleep properly, come tomorrow I am missing you.'

'Tomorrow is my operation day, Neelima, how shall I come tomorrow!'

'If you wont come, then I would come to Aligarh. I had been missing you, you couldn't imagine',

Neelima told him.'

'Don't come to Aligarh,' Pradeep was afeared of her coming to Aligarh, Vibha would make him fluid by making innumerable pieces of his torso,

'Any way I am coming on Sunday.' He shuddered at the thought of Neelima arriving to Aligarh.

Vibha would create the scene, Pradeep was sure.

'Sunday is after too many days, I cant wait for so long, want your caresses on my body Pradeep try to understand and Pradeep I have fixed the operation of mammoplasty for wednesday, so eiher come tomorrow or any way you have to come on Wednesday,' Neelima reasoned with him.

'Neelima, how can I come on Wednesday!' He persisted.

'You have to come, come for me, come for patient,' She was complacent.

Unlocking the door he thrusted himself in the apartment. What to do, he was in dilemma. If vibha came to know, she would murder him. But he would not like to miss Wednsday's operation, first operation in Delhi. And he would get glimpses of Neelima this time may be of whole body, and he wont run this time, guide his organ deep in her cavern ecstatic one, and would caress her gently with his organ, caress her boobs caress her navel and caress her feminine flesh slowly very slowly until she would be aroused fiercely . . . Neelima a blossoming flower in a beautiful garden spreading the aroma of youth and he was mesmerized.

Pradeep went to the hospital when registrar told that the first case planned for the operation had been shifted to Operation room. He told registrar to prepare and drape the patient with sterile linen. After completing the operation he did laparoscopy of another patient to find out the status of the fallopian tubes which were blocked. Few cases were minor and Pradeep asked registrar to finish.

When he was in his chamber after the operations Vibha came. He told her that he had done microsurgical operation for impotency, Vibha applauded him.

'Vibha I shall go to Delhi tomorrow,' Pradeep told her huskily. 'Delhi,' she squeaked. 'For what reason?'

'Neelima had fixed mammoplasty for Wednesday,' he told her timidly.

'This witch will spoil you, no way. You wont go there,' Vibha told him sternly.

'Cool down,' Pradeep tried to pacify her, 'I am not going to meet Neelima, certainly not. Iwill go straight to nursing home, complete the operation and come back.'

'In that case, I will go with you,' Vibha was determined.

'What!' his eyes were wide. 'Why will you waste your time?' He asked huskily.

'I am wary of the witch Neelima. I will go with you,' she was firm.

If she goes with me, how I shall caress her breasts. Ok, I shall caress her boobs in next visit perhaps, and introduce her as his assistant and inform Neelima in advance so that nothing goes beresek. Or do something else, this arrangement is not ok, he will not be able to see her naked boobs . . . No Vibha I can not not take you along with me. Will not take you with me, you will be sleeping and I will go to Delhi, Pradeep grinned to himself.

This time she would not allow him to go to Neelima, she was intelligent and would play smarter than him, Vibha thought and walked out the chamber.

Vibha woke up early in the morning and hurriedly got showered herself. Putting on yellow saree she took out a hand bag and walked out of her apartment. Incidentally Pradeep also came out at the same time. 'Good morning Pradeep ji, I have played smarter today, you couldn't have left me again.' Pradeep grinned to himself. She had played smarter that day. His longing for Neelima would not be fulfilled that day. Her naked thighs, naked boobs, he was sure to gloat at across in bathroom, Vibha had spoiled the whole programme. Her thighs like banana tree, glistening over which his eyes would slip down or up to the raven black tuft of hair carefully protecting the feminine knob of flesh which could turn a male to fluid and longing for having a glimpse of feminine beauty deep inside after freezing and becoming hard like frozen ice to become fluid again by the warmth of her flesh.

When both of them disembarked from the train at station, Neelima was standing at a distance just few meters away. She spotted Pradeep and came hurrying up, 'Hello.'

Pradeep shook her hand and introduced Vibha to her, 'She is Vibha.'

Neelima did not take notice of her and gave a powerful kiss to Pradeep. Vibha staggered, angered and her face flushed, the witch, kissing in public, she knew she had enticed my man; fingers twitched fist was made and heart raced at fast pace.

Neelima casted a casual glance at her and walked to exit with Pradeep, Vibha following her. She did not like the behaviour of Neelima, her suscipicion was proved right, the way she had shook his hand, something is going on in her heart, and her dress, her buttocks are visible shamelessly above the waist of the jeans; should it be the way to wear the jeans and the shirt, transparent, everything was visible through that even her black bra. She is the witch. How to save my man from her clutches.

Neelima entered the car unlocking the door and opend both doors for Pradeep and Vibha from inside. Pradeep sat on the front seat by side of Neelima, Vibha occupied the rear seat.

Everybody was tense in car, Vibha did not like her dress, too provocative for men to be aroused and her man was simple. Pradeep was tense as he was not able to ogle at her boobs which were seen through transparent yellow shirt as if white lily covered by yellowness of rising sun in the morning. He ogled at her swells and developed sudden desire to have the glimpse of those ecstatic swells without the protection of raivement. Vibha had spoilt all programmes.

Neelima stopped the car in front of Grover nursing home and asked Pradeep to get down, she would be joining after parking the car. Pradeep climbed down and waved Vibha also to follow him. He ascended the stairs and went to reception where she informed that patient had been shifted to the operation table, anesthetist had already come and everybody was waiting for you sir, Dr Pradeep.' 'Oh!' He turned to go to operation theatre with Vibha when Neelima also joined. He told that patient had apready shifted to operation theatre so he had to go in operation, what was her programme, he asked.

'How much time it would take in the operation?' Neelima asked.

'About two hours.'

'Alright, In that case I shall go to studio and come back after some time.'

'It is right,' Pradeep agreed and shook her hand. He kept on holding the hand for longer than required and Vibha noticed it. 'Let us hurry up,' she intervened. Neelima looked at her and smiled, 'Ok I am leaving,' she said and turned to go. Pradeep walked along with her to the car, Neelima clutched his hand, 'Pradeep I have started missing you. Why have you brought your assistant with you. She eyes me with anger, as if I am snatching her husband, is there something between you? Even if it is there forget it, Pradeep is for Neelima.'

'Leave her, Neelima, I miss you too,' Pradeep said and took her hand and guided that to his lips to give a kiss, she writhed, 'Pradeep, you would kill me.' After getting control of her, she said, 'Please wait and dont go anywhere. I shall try to come earlier,' said Neelima and unlocked the door. She brought hand out of the window and held his hand, guided upto her lips and kissed. 'I love you Pradeep.' The kiss of Neelima was too sensuous and he felt sudden rush of blood to engorge his organs.

Pradeep walked back leaving Neelima to reception where Vibha had become furious. 'Pradeep why are you after her, she is not good woman, see her dress even her buttocks are seen.'

'What is wrong in that dress!' Pradeep defended.

'Pradeep!' her eyes were wide in exclamation. 'You don't see any thing wrong with dress? So provocative!'

'Vibha, it is Delhi and she is model. For her these dresses are normal,' Pradeeop reasoned. 'Ok, come on let us go to operation theater.' Pradeep pulled her to go to operation theatre.

'She was shaking your hand!'

'Vibha what is wrong in that, internationally it is accepted mode of greeting any body,' Pradeep was bit irritated.

'Hey man, don't tell me international norms,' Vibha told him sternly. 'I rightly sensed that something was going on between you, had seen it; walking like a great film star, Huh, and showing every part of body, and Pradeep following her ogling at her protrusions.'

Pradeep burst in laughter listening to her comments.

'Don't laugh,' she was irritated.

Fighting they both entered the operation theatre complex. Pradeep entered the men's changing room and she in ladies changing. Both put on OT dresses.

The operation was complete within two hours, Pradeep came out of operation complex with Vibha putting on the regular clothes. Neelima was waiting in the chamber of Grover, she smiled sensuously finding Pradeep entering the chamber. 'I went to studio but missed you a lot, not feeling at ease, so came back,' said Neelima stooping over the table. As she stooped over her boobs were visble. It was maddening to Pradeep and Vibha both. Pradeep was mad with arousal when he felt pulsations of fast flow of blood to his masculine hardness and Vibha was mad with anger, how could she say that she was not feeling at ease becase she was missing Pradeep, the witch.

'She had fallen in love for you,' commented Grover.

Pradeep hurriedly looked at Vibha.

'How is your patient?' she asked.

'Fine.'

'How much increase in size of breasts she would achieve?'

'Now she can bear 36 size bra.'

'Oh that's great,' Neelima applauded, 'Show me the pictures if you have taken, I am interested in the procedure because I know many of the girls in the industry who are not successful as they are not endowed with big boobs, and I might also opt for operation,' said she and giggled.

Why pradeep was so respectful to her, she was not assistant, there had to be something else; girl friend or finacee!Did not look like, Medico, they are moron, he could not pierce me inside, compelety moron, talked of moral value. What moral!if both adults were interested where was the question of immorality. Pradeep asked Neelima to accompany him to operation recovery room if she wanted to see the patients afterwards he would show the photographs also. Neelima acomanied him. 'Vibha just wait over here, Neelima wanted to see the patient which I had just operated.'

Vibha nodded her head.

Pradeep guided Neelima to the recovery room where the patient was lying over the bed. He removed the sheet from over her operated bosom. Neelima was aghast, 'My god, such big size!Pradeep perform surgery over me also.'

'Your's are of ideal shape and size,' Pradeep yelled passing through the corridor.

'How do you know?' Neelima quizzed turning her head a bit in direction of Pradeep and in one lonely corner she tilted her head little up pouting her lips inviting him to snog at her. Pradeep became nervous and hurriedly snogged at her wanted to be away immediately but Neelima was faster and held his head to keep lips of both interlocked for long.

Pradeep was dancing at the feminine soft tune of Neelima.

They entered the chamber of Grover to whom she told that Dr Pradeep had done commendable job.

'Yes, he is talented plastic surgeon', Grover agreed. He ordered for tea. 'Dr Pradeep any specific instructions for postoperative care of the patient?' Grover asked.

'None, I will change her dressing on Sunday.'

'And you are coming on Sunday?'

'Yes.' After tea, Pradeep wrote down the postoperative orders, gave instructions to the nurse and went to examine the patient again, as she was alright, he came back to the chamber, and asked Neelima to move. Grover had left the chamber. Vibha automatically followed Pradeep.

Jostling with Pradeep Neelima strolled to car parking. Vibha was following them, **her body burning with anger, pulsating with flow of blood not to her feminine valley but to her face and hands.** She should beat him with sandals and that witch also. Look they were walking as teenager lovers. What to say the witch, Pradeep, he had also become mad.

Car was racing when at times Pradeep jostled with Neelima at turns, mere touch of her boobs was sensuous. Vibha was minutely observing. Neelima stopped the car at the same restarant where they had taken lunch before also, all three entered the restaurant, Neelima was not much happy, an assistant should not take lunch with them. She ordered for lunch and asked, 'Pradeep will there be scar?'

'Minute hidden in inframammary crease.' Neelima was sitting in front of Pradeep and Vibha was sitting by his side. He was gloating at the beautifully carved boobs, which Vibha was not liking. This witch had made my man her doggy, I have to do something.

After lunch they went to the house of Neelima.

At a turn as she turned the car Pradeep fell over Neelima and he hurriedly kissd her left thigh, kiss was so sensuous that Neelima felt waves inside her body, inside her ecstatic valley.

She stopped the car in front of the gate and moved inside the house with Pradeep and Vibha. Neelima asked, 'Are you staying tonight?'

'No.'

'Why?'

'There is nobody in the department, so I have to reach in the evening,' Pradeep reasoned.

'Ok, it is 3 and Magadh express train would leave at 7 in evening, so there is still 3 hours time with you. So you can realx, come upstairs. Once on first floor she asked Vibha to rest in the room adjacent to that of Pradeep. 'You can relax over here,' Neeelima told Vibha, she was uncertain, was not sure what Pradeeo had told her about their relations. Neelima entered her room and Pradeep in his.

Pradeep changed the clothes and lay on the bed when Neelima came.

'Pradeepl miss you a lot,' Neelima pleaded sitting by his side. 'I don't know what had happened to me, wish you could have stayed tonight,' she requested clutching his hand and caressing his masculine and coarser hair on forearm with her nubile fingers. Hair felt the feminine warmth and slowly became erect. Neelima smiled, 'Feel your hair are erect.' Pradeep took her in his embrace and put his lips over hers, 'And so is by masculinity.'

'Useless masculinity, what a masculinity when you cant love the feminity, when you run from the scene while feminine valley aspires for you.' Pradeep looked at her and smiled.

'I love youPradeep, cant live without you, come to Delhi now you are getting the patients also,' she requested kissing his forearm and erect hair.

'I love you too, you are my heart throb, was spell bound by your bewitching smile, when I saw you for the first time in Aligarh, I fell In love for you, since then.'

'Then what is the hitch in coming to Delhi?' she asked, putting her fingers over his lips as if tryng to explore something.

'I am planning to shift.' he said, 'I have to shift.' He suddenly took her in embrace again.

'Come Pradeep, come. Dont worry for any thing, I have big house for stay and will give you lot of patients, girls in modelling need lot of cosmetic surgery to improve their appearance; however they don't know where to go, I shall guide them,' Neelima clutched his hand and put over her boobs. This moron doctor would not do any thing. Pradeep cupped her protrusions and caressed slowly while Neelima was caressing his mighty chest. Pradeep was caressing both of her boobs which caused the buttons of the shirt to fall down and both boobs becoming peel free. He was stunned to see the beauty of heaven on the earth.

His hand slipped fom the breast down over her abdomen and from there to her rounded buxom hips, he was hungrily trying to eat Neelima who kissed him fiercely and she in frenzied ecstasy got hold of his masculine organ, his body was embered. She got hold of Pradeep hand and put over her silken tuft of hair and thrusted down. Moron do something she spelled to her self and suddenly she pulled down her clothes and put his organ over her valley's entrance and she was about to thrust so that it entered, sombody knocked at the door . . . both were bewildered.

Neelima separated and hurriedly went to the bathroom. Vibha entered when Pradeep opened the door. 'Come,' he said.

'Why did you not open the door immediately?' she asked and glanced through the room. Pradeep was tense, he hurriedly came out, 'Out side is very pleasant let us enjoy the evening,' he almost pulled Vibha out.

This bloody assistant, she is not leaving Pradeep. Oh my God, My body is burning, what to do, I have to do it myself now.

'It is 5 pm, after one hour we shall go, You will come again on Sunday?' Vibha asked. She was puzzled why Pradeep had pulled her outside. Was Neelima there insdie room and had hideen in bathroom. She should go inside bathroom.

'Yes.'

'I will also come.'

'For what?'

'I can not leave you alone,' she said and turned to go to room of Pradeep. 'Let me wash my hands.'

Pradeep was bewildered. She had to be prevented from going to his room. Vibha was not relenting and almost running entered the bath room. But there was nobody inside.

Pradeep was waiting for her outside was sure of fiasco, a fight between two ladies. He should run. At same time Vibha came out side. But why she was not in bad mood. No cries, no fights.

'Washed hands?'

'Yes.'

'In bathroom?'

'Why are you asking me, there was somebody hidden in the bathrrom?'

'Who, who was there?' Pradeep was trembling.

'There was nobody, but why are you perspiring?'

'Me . . . no no . . . i am not.'

Pradeep was not normal. There must be Neelima hidden somewhere whom she could not catch. Vibha was thinking.

Getting relieved Neelima went to her room while their back was towards the gate of the room. My God this assistant was fast woman, there was something between them. Whatsoever was there now Pradeep was hers.

At six Neelima came out of the room and found Vibha and Pradeep sitting on parapet. 'Ok let us go down, have tea and move, I will drop you to station.' Neelima suggested. She was envious of Vibha, assistant sitting in close proximity to Pradeep, there was definitely something more, and she had to act fast, otherwise she would snatch Pradeep from her.

Pradeep went to his room and asked Vibha also to get prepared. After tea In the evening Neelima dropped them at railway station and kissed Pradeep in front of Vibha. Her eyes were wide in exasperation, in anger and desbelief, both were burning inside for same reasons.

Chapter 8

Train was about to leave when Vibha and Pradeep entrained. Neelima waved her hand, Pradeep was at the gate waving to her, when she was no longer in sight, he came back and sat with Vibha.

'Now you are in train with me, better you would have stayed with her,' Vibha commented sarcastically.

Pradeep looked at her but said nothing, he was In melancholy mood, Neelima had mesmerized him, and he started missing her, developed love for her, developed longing for her, and she (Vibha) was passing sarcasm. She would not understand the true love which he had developed for her.

Train was running at fast speed and both were silent. What had happened to Vibha, she had become envious of hers beauty. Why pradeep was so much after Neelima, only for her charm, **body of a woman could make any man mad for her**; my man was lost in her, what to do, Vibha was thinking. There was something growing up between Pradeep and Neelima, but he was trying to hide from her. He was not profligate person but innocent it was all due to Neelima who was modern and took advantage of him. She had to do something lest she would lose Pradeep, he was being befooled by Neelima—the witch, what she had put on was beyond her imagination, jeans so short at waist that her buttocks and panty were visible, shamefull indeed, she was peering out.

Train stopped at Aligarh railway station when both of them got down and riding on a cycle ricksaw went to the residential campus, Pradeep went with vibha to her apartment and then came back to his. He was so tired that he lay on sofa even without opening the shoe strings and shoes on.

What to do, he was in embriligo. Vibha was a good girl but not sexy sensuous, Neelima was really sensuous, mere sight of whom was enough to make his hair stand erect.

But he did not want to lose vibha either, she was a good girl, however Neelima was superb. At Delhi what ever had happened would have aroused the suscipicion in her mind and he had to be careful.

He got to his toes, why should he worry for Vibha, he was not going to mary her and he had to tell it, sooner it was told better it would be. He would marry Neelima, she was also In love for him, If he married to her, he would settle in Delhi, big house and erotic body of a woman. Pradeep was taken away by Neelima and suddenly he started missing her, so he dialled her number and called her. 'How are you Neelima?' He asked, 'I am missing you.'

'Pradeep,' she gave a kiss, 'it reached to you?' She asked.

He also kissed and said your kiss was sexy and he was aroused. 'Oh Pradeep! don't make me aroused again, I would become mad, too many times you have left me burning, on embers. No man should do it too a woman. I wanted your juices to calm me down but you ran away, why had you brought her, asistant, don't bring her again, she was suscipicious of us throughout the whole day as if she was your girl friend. Ok you are coming on Sunday, but tell me how to live for three full days, Pradeep, this time don't go soon. Come on Sunday and stay on Monday, we would enjoy Pradeep. I long for you, your body, your sex and everything yours, Pradeep don't go back this time on Sunday.'

Pradeep went to hospital the next day and opened his chamber, when registrar came. Pradeep told him that he would like to inspect the dressing of impotent patient. Registrar went to the ward for opening the dressing of Impotent patient. Afer some time Pradeep went to the ward and inspected the dressing. 'How are you?' He asked.

'I am fine doctor.'

'Okay if everything is alright we would discharge you in few days,' Pradeep informed.

'Thanks doctor.'

He came back to his chamber. Vibha did not come, though he was waiting fot her to come. Why he was waiting for Vibha, he asked to him self, he was not marrying to her, in which case he should tell her plainly that he was not marrying to her; and their relation then would be finished.

He did not like her physically, never liked her, but why he was missing her, for example that day why he was missing her. His head was aching so he locked the chamber and went to the apartment. That has never happend before, what to do, how to come out of fiasco—on one side was Vibha and on other Neelima.

Neelima was stunning beauty and Vibha average looking woman . . . Strolling to the bed room he lay on the bed. His head was having severe ache so he was thumping forehead with the heel of the palm, when he listened to the giggling sounds coming out from nearby apartment. He sat on the bed and tried to listen it patiently, as sounds were not audible he went upstairs and peered out into the apartment down. Mrs Maheshwari was there with Dr Gupta in compromising posture . . .

The witch, Pradeep abused her and came down. The words said once by Vibha echoed in his mind—beautiful women are source of trouble for husbands . . .

In the evening he started missing Vibha, so he went to her apartment. Vibha opened the gate. 'Yes, what do you want?' She asked sternly. Pradeep was taken aback. 'There is no place for you in this apartment,' Vibha roared.

Vibha tried to close the door after him, but Pradeep enterd inside thrusting her aside, she looking at him helpless.

'What do you want Pradeep?' Vibha was stern.

'Please sit down,' Pradeep requested her to sit.

'I am just asking for what reasons you have come over here in my apartment. Go to Neelima.

'Truth is that you have been infatuated by Neelima, every man would have fallen for her body, you are no different,' she was stern.

'What do you mean?'

'Pradeep, you think your self very smart, I can accept every excuse of yours, but how should I accept your kissing over her thighs; too much disgusting, and that too in my presence, in front of me you have kissed her as if I would not be able to see and over her thighs.'

Pradeep was stunned at her revelation that she knew that he kissed her, her anger was perfect then and she had perfect right in not allowing him to enter her apartment.

'Just caressed her boobs In the room, Pradeep ji, I should have slapped you over there, unfortunately I am not smart, not brave. I could not do any thing just mere spectator, watching my man doing all nasty things to the woman. Too disgusting, nothing could be meaner than this. Now you get out immediately, get out,' she scaremed with full lung power. Pradeep remorsefully got up and walked out to reach his apartment.

He was not in good mood so he walked to the nearby park where he found a bench and let himself occupy that. Vibha had flurried, smashed him in pieces, Vibha who had been clinging to him for fifteen years, had throttled him.

Moon was in its full youth, large rounded and big orb, one day he had compared the face of Neelima with full moon and she was more attractive than moon. He got up and strolled in the park, Neelima was no doubt very attractive, he wanted his wife to be beautiful, Vibha was nowhere in comparision. He had to decide fast. Vibha had thrown him out, Neelima was also suspicipious of her. But Vibha was very intelligent, perhaps in these matters all women are alike. She had seen me kissing at her thighs and also her boobs . . .

Strolling he went to the far end of the park, suddenly he spotted somebody coming out of Gupta's apartment, he tried to figure out the person, but could not do it because of darkness, and when he could make out, he almost lost his control and sat down over the green grass.

Pradeep opened his chamber when the registrar came for the round.

'Are the patients alright?'

'Yes sir.'

'Any dressings to be done?'

'No sir.'

'Then take the round of the patients, I am not feeling well,' Pradeep told.

'Something wrong sir?' He asked.

'Slight headache.'

'Ok sir.'

Pradeep was not feeling well, memories of the night were haunting him, the way Vibha retaliated and insulted him was nightmare for him.

But she was right, how a girl would tolerate his man kissing another woman over thighs, over boobs; but he was also not wrong, he had never promised to marry her or expressed his desire for her. He always wanted a beautiful girl as his wife, sexy, big boobs, big posteriors. He fell for Neelima the day he saw her, his fault was that he had not told Vibha that he did not love her. However, she did not know the relations between them. If it was not love than what it was.

Two girls came in, both in their teens.

'Yes, how can I help you?'

'Sir we have come from Agra.'

'Please take the seat,' Pradeep offerd the chair.

'Sir,' girl on the right started hesitatingly, 'She is my friend, her boy friend disrobed her of womanhood and she is going to be married the coming month, I have heard that you perform the operation to restore virginity.'

'Yes I am doing the operation which has actually been described in the world by Dr Vishwa Prakash, I learnt from him and perform it, It can be done, come to my OPD on Monday,' Pradeep told.

'Sir, we have come from agra and wanted to get it performed today so that we may go back tomorrow.'

'Alright, but it will be done in nursing home, and there it would be expensive.'

'We have brought the money sir.'

'In that case go to Mittal nursing home and get admitted, I would perform the operation in the evening.'

They agreed and walked out of the chamber.

It was time for taking tea with Vibha, he started missing her.

In the evening he went to the apartment of Vibha, knocked at the door when Vibha opened the door. She was in sullen mood, face being withered, he skipped a heart beat, but she was in usual fury.

'Dr Pradeep what do you want?'

He kept mum.

'Vibha asked again,' Pradeep I cant allow our relations to go on this way.'

'Let me come inside,' Pradeep pleaded.

Vibha was not in mood to let him in, however she made room for him to enter. He walked to drawing and sat on sofa, Vibha followed him closing the door on her back and sat opposite to him.

'Vibha I am sorry,' Pradeep said huskily.

'Sorry for what? For kissing at her thighs or her boobs?' Vibha passed sarcastic comment.

'I am sorry for that Vibha, it was not my fault, she seduced me,' Pradeep stammered.

'Don't try to be smart, she seduced and the great plastic surgeon could not contain himself, and that was in front of me,' she roared like lioness, 'How could you dare to kiss her on her thighs in front of me, in front of me who has stuck to you for fifteen years. You did not feel shame even for a second, and today you are trying to prove your innocence; it is too much. I know you have developed lust for her body, you have to choose between lust and love, Neelima and Vibha. If you are really sorry forget her and marry to me, If you are agreed for this arrangement, I would again call my father and fix a date for marriage.'

Pradeep was again confused and bewildered, 'Vibha, I agree I developed lust for her body, because her body is superb, gorgeous glowing beauty, but it is neither lust or love for her, she is helping me to establish in Delhi,' Pradeep tried to reason with her.

'Oh, as she is helping you to settle in Delhi so her body has appealed to you, and what a shame you are describing her, gorgeous glowing beauty, I should slap you and tear you in pieces—glowing beauty. Dont you have little bit of self esteem . . . shame ful, shameful!'

'Vibha as love is concernd, Pradeep loves only Vibha,' he got up and kneeled before her, 'Vibha I love you.'

She became emotional. His kneeling before her, made her emotional, my man kneeling, she came in embrace of Pradeep, 'Pradeep I cant live without you, could not sleep for two days, I love you a lot.' Haze appeared due to saline water overflowing her eyes, 'Prdaeep I don't want to lose you, she is not good girl, the witch, you are very simple, Pradeep, innocent. Forget Delhi, we will settle in Aligarh. Life in Delhi is too complicated, no importance to moral values, ethics and interpersonal relations. Everything is wine wealth and women.'

Pradeep wiped the saline water from her eyes, 'Vibha I love you too. Forget Neelima and what had happened, It is mens'weakness for women. Give me a weeks'time and we would fix the date for marriage,' he lowered his face and caressed her cheeks, slowly coming to the lips and took her lower lips between his, lowering his lips over her neck and from there to boobs, when she prevented him to go further, 'After marriage.'

Back in the apartment Pradeep was confused, in dilemma, what to do and come out of this imbroglio. How could he marry vibha. He had kissed her, but there was no sensuality involved, did not have rush of blood to make his organ stiff, while mere kiss over the thighs of Neelima made him vibrate with hard organ which he could control with difficulty.

For marriage also lust had been important, otherwise sexual life would go haywire. Vibha was not able to arouse passion inside him.

He sat on sofa opened the shoestrings and pushed the shoes aside, kept his legs over the table, sexual involvement did not mean sexual act, he had hardly touched Vibha for fifteen years. Somtimes kissed but no further. However Neelima was always passionate, how could he forget her, who had made him experience the sensuality of female body, he was in love for her and not the lust. Night was blossoming, he casted a glance at the watch, it was 12 o'çlock. Vibha was also awake. Its not his fault, Vibha was thinking, a bare body of a woman could make any man mad for sex. Even the great saints like Vishwamitra could not control themselves, our man is placid. She was sure he loved her, if that was not so, he would not have come that day.

Pradeep went to hospital and went to take the round of the patients. He told the registrar that he might be on leave on Monday so he should take care of OPD. For operations for Tuesday he should put abdominoplasty as the first case. After the round he came to the chamber when Vibha came. 'I have got the information that our paper has ben accepted for the conferece,' told Pradeep and suggested that she should start preparing.

'OK, but you have to help me,' she requested.

'I am always for your help,' he winked and took Vibha in his embrace, she caressed his chest and the coarse and thick hair over there.

Pradeep put his finagers over her lips and moved from one to other slowly he pushed that over boobs, when Vibha was oblivious of that. When she realized, she shriekd, 'Cheat,' and got hold of his hand. 'No not permitted. I am not Neelima—the whore. She can get kisses over the boobs from a person whom she barely knows, I can call her a whore that's all.'

'Pradeep we should go to see a movie in the evening,' she proposed to which Pradeep agreed.

In the evening they went to the theatre to see a movie which was a story of the house which was headed by a widow, when his son was married, the tussle started with his wife.

Returning from movie Pradeep asked, 'Why does it happen?'

'What?'

'The mother in law who cherished the desire to bring the bride for his son, suddnely started behaving in devilish way, once the bride had come.'

Vibha did not answer. While leaving Vibha at her apartment he told that he had to go to Delhi next day morning, it was essential as he had to do dressing of the patient, however he assured that he wont meet Neelima, directly go to nursing home, do dressing, examine the patient if any new patient was there and come back, in the evening; he assured that he would follow his promise and she should believe in his words.

Pradeep got up early in the morning and hurriedly tidying up went to the railway station, as there was time in train to come, he strolled to tea shop and ordered for tea.

He had promised to Vibha that he would not meet Neelima, but would it be possible.

Neelima was Neelima and she was his heart throb. Tea was served so he lifted the cup and took a sip, main problem was how to wriggle out of the complex situation, he did not want to leave Vibha, but wanted to marry Neelima.

Train arrived so he entered the train josting with the crowd.

Vibha was too intelligent and clever, she had observed minutely what had transpired between Neelima and him.

At station he glanced round to find Neelima. She was no where in sight, suddeny from somewhere Neelima appeared. Dressed in black knee length skirt flanked by red shirt, she was appearing sensuous. The shirt was trying to cover her boobs which were wriggling to come out . . . and he developed an impulse to cup them.

'Neelima you are superb,' he said. She looked at him and giggled.

Pradeep followed her looking at her glabrous legs which were having glistening skin. She unlocked the door of car and entered. Pradeep entered from other side and sat beside her.

She did not start the car immediately.

Pradeep looked at her to find out the reasons for her not starting the car.

'Pradeep I missed you a lot. You did not even phone me, did not remember me while I was dying for you, missing you a lot and you didnot remember me at all. Did your assistant prevent you?'

'Which?'

'Same girl who had come with you last time.'

'Nothing like that, I was actually too busy.'

'And forgot Neelima,' she said and started the car which moved through the crowded streets of Cannaugt place.

'Neelima,' he kept his palm over her left thigh, 'I am sorry.'

Neelima felt his hand over thighs, feel of masculine hand over the thighs made hair over leg and thighs to be sensuous and respond by being engorged and erect. Pradeep had become smarter. His fingers were caressing her thigh up and down. Neelima was too aroused and unable to control the rising passion she removed his hand, 'Not here.'

She took the car in a byelane and reclined on the seat, clutched his hand and put over her thighs. He caressed the thigh which was sending innumerable waves inside him to cause his organ to become stiff. He caught hold of her hand and guided it to his stiff organ.

'Waho,' she praised. 'Pradeep I think we should move to the house in the protected structure of the house we should indulge, here we may not be able to control ourselves.'

She stopped the car and entered the house with Pradeep and asked Pradeep to relax a bit upstairs and then she would call him for breakfast. 'You also come,' he said clutching her hand and pulling her over the stairs.

She grinned, 'Shall come within no time,' she winked.

How could he leave her, yesternight he was in mood to forget Neelima, but she aroused so much passion inside him that he could not forget her, her thighs are so sensuous and skin was so sliky, it was gliding up his fingers to her valley, feminine and hot valley.

He put on the clothes brought up for Delhi and mountained down. 'Oooh!' she was in ecstacy, 'You are looking superb.' He had put on raven black shirt and white pant, combination was giving extra ordinary charming look to Pradeep.

He sat on sofa and lifted a news paper kept over there, when mother of Neelima came, 'How are you, my son?'

'I am fine,' he said.

'Where is Neelima?' She asked glancing alaround to find her.

'She was here just few seconds back, might have gone inside,' Pradeep told her.

'Come for breakfast,' she invited him as the breakfast was served on the table.

'Let her come, mom,' he said.

Neelima came down clad in black skirt which was shorter, flanked by green mini shirt, through which whole of her abdomen was visible. She was braless also as he could see the naked flesh of her protrusions and also . . . . the tiny knob of feminine flesh sitiuated at the ecstatic peak of protrusions.

'Come for breakfast, please,' Neelima asked him to come to breakfast table. He got up looking at her swaggering gait. She sat beside Pradeep and served omelette to him, he looked at her with a smile spread over face. 'Pradeep you are not only a great Plastic surgeon, but handsome too, try your luck in modelling.'

Pradeep smiled. Finishing the breakfast Neelima came out with Pradeep, unlocking the door of car Neelima entered into the driver's seat and Pradeep sat on passenger's seat beside her.

'So today what is the programme?' He asked and paused before praising her, 'Your skirt is very sensuous, causing something deep inside me.'

'Doctor don't tell me, when I offered you my sexuality, you just ran away. Are doctors so moron? I can shed off my skirt here, you should be bold enough to do, don't close your eyes, or run away,' she laughed roaring.

She parked the car at same secluded place and clutching his hand put over her thigh, which aroused Pradeep and he suddenly embraced her, lowered his face to kiss all over her face. After some time she started the car, 'Pradeep I miss you a lot so now make the plan to come to Delhi.'

Car stopped in the parking area of Grover's nursing home, both got down to go to main building of the nursing home.

Receptionist told that patient was waiting for the dressing.

'Oh she is in time.'

'Pradeep, Mrs Dixit has also come, let us see her before you go for changing the dressing of the patient.' Pradeep followed Neelima to the chamber where Mrs Dixit was waiting, 'Hello Mrs dixit, you are in time,' said Neelima entering the chamber, then she introduced Pradeep to her, 'He is Dr Pradeep great plastic surgeon.' Then she turned to Pradeep, 'Pradeep I forgot to tell you on the way, Mrs Dixit is interested in mammoplasty, she had talked to me a day before.'

'She praised about you a lot,' Mrs Dixit told him and lifted her hand to shake his hand.

'She is interested in meeting the patient on whom you have done mammoplasty,' Neelima told Pradeep.

He called nurse and asked to shift the patient of mammoplasty to dressing room. 'Patient is in dressing room, sir,' nurse told Pradeep.

He got up and told Mrs Dixit, 'I shall call you, when dressing is done and then you can talk to her.'

He inspected the dressing, every thing was well healed, he removed the stitches and called nurse to call Mrs Dixit to come inside. Nurse called Mrs Dixit and told her Dr Pradeep was calling to meet the patient. Dixit got to her toes and went to meet the patient on whom the mammoplasty was done. She was impressed with the result,' Oh, that's great, Dr Pradeep I am waititing for you to examine me and fix the date of operation, 'Mrs Dixit was impressed by the spectacular result of mammoplasty, so large and so natural, prodding, as that of a virgin.'

'I will examine just now,' Pradeep told her and then asked the nurse to guide her in the examination room.

He examined Mrs Dixit and told her that your bra size is 28 which was too small, he could give her a huge size.'

'42?'

'Yes 42, I will give you size of 42.'

'Is it really possible!' She squeaked.

'Yes,' Pradeep told her plainly.

'Ok doctor in that case fix the date of operation,' she requested.

'Next Sunday,' Pradeep suggested.

'That's fine with me.'

Neelima also came over there and overheard their conversation. She told Pradeep, 'Do it tomorrow.'

'Yes, I am fine if you do tomorrow,' Mrs Dixit agreed.

Pradeep agreed for the operation the next day.

He discharged the mammoplasty patient to whom he advised to massage her breasts thrice a day with flat of palm, it is essential otherwise the capsule forms around breast which may contract—resulting in capsular contracture. He called her up for follow up on the next Sunday.

Pradeep remained over there for amost one hour, as none of the patient came Neelima offered,' Let us go for coffee, nurse would inform if some patients comes.'

While in car Neelima suggested,' Plan for the operation tomorrow, you would get many patients,' she clutched his hand.

She stopped the car in front of the restaurant, 'What are the complications of the surgery,' getting down from the car she asked.

'Mainly two-infection and capsular contracture.'

Inside the restaurant almost all tables were unoccupied so Neelima walked over to a table at far end of restaurant, out of sight of persons. Occupying the chair she continued, what would happen if infection took place?'

'Antibiotics are given, but infection is not very common, we take all precations that it should not occur.'

Waiter came for taking the order, Neelima orderd for two coffee.

'And what if contracture develops?'

'Contracture results in deformity, if minor, it is released through a small operation, if very severe, implant has to be removed, capsule is removed and implant is put again.' Pradeep told.

Waiter placed the mugs on the table. 'How about me opting for breast implant surgery?'

Pradeep looked at her, his eyes wide. 'You are endowed with well developed bosom, must be 36 size of bra fitting to your breasts.'

'Yes, make it 38.'

Pradeep smiled, 'Ok.'

After coffee Neelima returned home with Pradeep and asked Prdaeep to go upstairs and relax. 'We would take lunch at about 1pm, is that OK?'

Pradeep nodded and mountained up the stairs, though he was in no mood to separate from Neelima.

She was superb in every dress, or without protective covering, her every inch of body was maddening, he was thinking mountaining up. He wanted his wife like Neelima, gorgeous and beautiful, a nymph; whose every part of body was maddening to him. Upstairs he turned to the room he had occupied before also, there was no lock so opening the door he entered and lay on the bed. Vibha and Neelima; they would make him mad. he had to take a decision, indecisiveness would cause problems.

Maid came to call for lunch after some time. He got up, washed the face towelled and came down.

Neelima was already on dining table. Her father and mother also joined.

'Mama he had done fantastic operation, increased the size of boobs of a flat chested girl, so natural looking,' she told to mother, who was happy,' He is nice plastic surgeon, 'Pradeep, son take care of her, she is too innocent.'

'Pradeep now mother has also asked to take my care, so you cant refuse,' Neelima commented and giggled.

'Who does not want to take your care?' Asked Pradeep.

After lunch pradeep went to his room upstairs and lay on bed, was awakened by Neelima. She was clad in red skirt flanked by black shirt, her thighs emanating out of red skirt to give spenderous look as if two gynadra hanging from red rose flower. He could not control himself and took her in embrace, putting his hand over her posterior protrusions and moving the fingers from one side to other as if trying to explore some thing, she was aroused and pressed his head against her boobs; kneading the posterior protrusions his hand ascended over the waist and back and then neck to come anteriorly over her protrusions and kissed over her boobs.

At the same time maid knocked at the door, 'Phone call for you madam.'

She drifted away, 'Nonesense.'

Neelima went out and Pradeep lay on the bed, he did not like the interference by maid when they were engaged in dalliance activity, his body was raging with passionate desire. Neelima returned within few minutes and informed that call was from Mrs Dixit and she had confirmed the operation for next day. 'Will you like to go somehere in evening?'

'Where?'

'Boat club.'

'No.'

'Then?'

'Somewhere else.'

'Where?'

'Lodhi garden, I have heard a lot about it.'

'Ok,' Neelima agreed.

Pradeep got up after one our and walked to the bathroom. Splashing sounds were emanating from the adjacent bath room, he longed to look at the naked body of Neelima but did not dare to ascend up on the stool. Neelima came after half an hour, 'Let us move,' she proposed. She was in white salwar suit as if whilte lily flower or a white rose in front of which a petal of red rose was lying. The red rose, like her luscious blossoming libidinous lips; and he put his lips over hers,' you are appearing as white rose flower.

She burst in laughter, 'Oh! you are poet as well.'

'No I am not poet, any man would become poet sighting a gorgeous and immensely beautiful woman like you.' His lips were wandering over hers.

'Hidden poet in you.'

After sometimes they parted away and Neelima asked him to come down. Pradeep would prove a good husband, she was thinking, doctor handsome with well built body.

Putting on the regular clothes Pradeep came down and both entered in the car. Neelima started the car and took left turn to come on the road 'Pradeep perform the mammoplasty of Mrs Dixit, then examine me also, I want furthur enlargement,' she persuaded him.

'I will examine you in the evening.'

'Where?'

'In room?'

'Will you be able to examine?'

'Why not?'

She giggled. 'I have no problem, you are the doctor.'

At Lodi garden she stopped the car and got out Pradeep mountaining down from other side.

Neelima clutched his hand and chose a place in the garden behind a shrub out of the sight of general public. She sat on the grass and rested her head against his shoulder. 'I love you Pradeep.' She expressed.

'I love you too, Neelima,' Pradeep answered raking his finger in her hair.

'You don't love me,' Neelima rebuked him softly.

'How can you say that?'

'If you had love for me, you would have come to Delhi,' Neelima said caressing coarse hair onhis mighty chest.

'Would come,' told Pradeep cupping her face with his hands and peeping into her eyes.

'Pradeep come to Delhi other wise I will not be able to live without you', Neelima said resting her head in his lap, her boobs rubbing his thighs, which was too ecstatic.

She drawled. 'Pradeep I love you.'

Both returned to home after sometime, father and mother were waiting for them; father objected for them coming home late, 'Neelima you should be careful of time.'

'I am so sorry dad.'

Mother said, 'My son take care of her'

She giggled, 'Pradeep take care of me.'

After dinner Pradeep went to his room upstairs.

Neelima went to her room and put on the grey nighty which was having the string just below the breasts to make them more protuberant.

She walked to the room of Padeep and called him to come outside. In the moon light Neelima was glittering, She clutched his hand and strolled to one end of verandah to sit over parapet.

Pradeep was looking at moon.

'Pradeep look at the moon,' Neelima said.

'Not as beautiful as you are.' he praised.

She burst in laughter, 'Pradeep try your luck in poems,' she suggested.

'And who would do plastic surgery? Poems cant earn me a living here in India,' Pradeep was in melancholic mood. He had inherent and god gifted virtue of a poet but had no time to express his creative ability in the form of poems.

He clutched her hand and kissed. 'Neelima, I love you, want to leave Aligarh and flee to you.'

'That's what I also want. I cant live without you, always miss you a lot,' said Neelima peering out.

The night was slight colder. The sky was studded with stars as if they were celebrating the union of night with the earth—union of two lovers, which everybody love. Cold breeze was caressing their bodies as if two lovers were trying to interwind with each other. Neelima clutched his hand and took him in her room, hugging him, she yelled, 'Pradeep I love you too much,' and stamped a kiss over his cheeks.

The kisses were so sensuous that Pradeep was aroused, he caressed her cheeks slowly and meekly fingers decending down and went beneath the protective covering on her body and over her carved out protuberances. She was in frenzy, while his fingers were searching her protuernaces slowly and slowly, as if trying to find out some thing, as if trying to find out the explicit carvings of God on her body, as if mesemrized by charm of exquitste carvings, and went on moving the finger tips slowly all over the carvings, all around the carvings and all along the carvings; unable to find out the depth of carvings his fingres ascended on the ecstatic cliff, snow covered cliff of a mountain, but it was warm, it was hot, and it was pulsating, Neelima was in trance,' Pradeep your finger tips are making me mad. Oooh!' she groaned and hugged him more firmly and as soon as he was going to enter inside her valley, his morality usurped, and he drifted away running to his room, 'Not before marrige.'

Neelima was maddened, in an attack of anger she went to his room and slapped him, 'Impotent male, you are not fit to be loved . . .'

Chapter 9

Pradeep opened the chamber and went inside, kept the bag on the side table when registrar came for taking him to the round of the patients.

'How are the patients?' he asked.

'All patients are alright, tuboplasty patient is also alright, her bowel sounds are audible so I have advised her to take liquids.'

He turned and asked the registrar to take the round of all the patients, he had to prepare for Fem Gen Con conference which was scheduled to take place in Pune.'

Registrar went out. Pradeep opened his laptop and powerpoint presentation and started working on it to prepare the Triple Flap Vaginoplasty.

Vibha came, 'Where were you Pradeep? You have gone for 1 day and did not come on Monday also, no phone call; Neelima would make you mad, disgusting, shift to delhi, Pradeep, nothing can help,' she was in full blown anger.

'Vibha, I told you over the phone that I had to operate a paient for breast enlargement.'

'And I have asked you to come to Aligarh and operate next Sunday,'

'Vibha try to understand, when the patient is ready for the operation . . .'

'Don't pretend operation, operation could have been done on Sunday, spell plainly that you were leering at her boobs or thighs, what had happened to to you, had become perfect womanizer. Its good you are getting the patients.'

'Believe me Vibha I have not snogged Neelima at thighs or at boobs.'

127

'Pradeep,' she caught his ear, 'I shall slap you with sandals. You have not kissed Neelima at thighs or boobs, how can you spell these words, and you are telling to me, to your would be wife . . .'

Pradeep grinned. 'I am preparing the power point presentation for Fem Gen Con conference.' he tried to change the topic of discussion.

'Hey don't change the topic, you have not answered why had you not come on Monday?'

Pradeep grinned again, 'Vibha let me develop practice of Plastic surgery in Delhi, we would shift to Delhi.

'I am not going anywhere and you would not go to Delhi any more,' Vibha was stern.

She got to her toes and went to the small kitchen space to prepare the tea and returned with tray having two cups.

'You should study, as paper has to be presented by you,' Pradeep suggested lifting one cup.

In the evening Pradeep went to the apartment of Vibha who was in sofa, books and journals lying over the table just to show that she was busy in study. Actually she was lost in thoughts where she would go for honeymoon.

'What are you doing?' asked Pradeep.

She kept mum.

'Are you preparing for the conference?'

'Yes,' said Vibha. He was happy that she was studying.

He strolled and sat in the sofa.

'Pradeep please check it,' Vibha requested stretching her hand to give him few papers.

He went through the papers and was satisfied.

'Look, I have become more intelligent now,' said Vibha and giggled.

Pradeep looked at her. Vibha flushed finding Pradeep looking at her, throbbiing arteries beneath her black skin could be felt by her. He kept his hand around her neck, Vibha came to senses, she yelled,' What are you doing!'

'What?'

'Why are you keeping your hand over my . . . my . . . ,' she mumbled and lifted the hand from over breasts, 'After marriage.'

Pradeep was in no mood to relent and cupped the boobs again. She was furious, 'Pradeep remove your hand. I don't like it.'

He grinned and smiled wickedly. Then he removed the hand from over her bosom and smiled 'Ok, after marriage.'

'Vibha we are reserving the flights to Pune on 6th October, is that ok with you?'

Vibha agreed, 'its ok with me.'

'And what about accommodation? One room would do?'

Her eyes were wide in exclamation, 'Pradeep, one room after marriage.'

He laughed. After some time they decided to go to Gandhi park a beautiful park having fountains, walking through which they sat on a bench, Vibha holding his hand pulled a bit and pointed to an younger couple who were kissing each other. Praddeep looked at the couple and holding the head of Vibha put his lips over hers, when she drifted her face away. 'After marriage,' she told him to kiss after marriage.

After sometime they returned back to apartment of Vibha where Pradeep lay on bed with a thud. Vibha went inside to take the bath. 'Pradeep, I am coming after bath, lot of humidity has drenched my body with sweat,'

Soon splashes were emanating from bathroom. Pradeep went to her bed room, when Vibha entered into bathroom, oblivious of presence of Pradeep over there in bedroom, suddenly she spotted him and immediately rushed back to the bathroom baffled by the presence of Pradeep in her bedroom, where she had entered naked after bath. Her blood was rushing at thunderous speed, body burning with shame and she was boiling in anger.

After sometime she cooled down and squeaked from inside the bath room, 'Pradeep how did you come in my room, go away from my bed room.'

'I am alone,' Pradeep answered in loud voice so that she could hear what he told.

'I say you get out,' she screamed.

Pradeep was not in mood to have confrontations and came out of bed room to drawing hall. Vibha opened the door and peeped into the room through the chink, sure that room was vacant she came out and lifting the saree from wardrobe put over her to wrap her nudity.

She was furious at his behaviour, he should not have come inside, should not behaved in this manner, it was her fault that she had not bolted the door from inside, but he should have behaved in gentlemens' way. She bolted the door this time towelled whole body and put on green saree.

Pradeep was remorseful, though it was not his intention to see her naked, he never thought she would come out of bathroom naked, he thought and kept on waiting for her to come out, she did not come, so he walked to her room again and called her from outside.

She kept mum.

He again called her, 'Vibha', he was expecting her not to answer.

'Vibha,' he again called. She opened the door when he entered inside and took her in embrace, 'Sorry Vibha.'

She tried to wriggle out when Pradeep clutched her more firmly and insinuated his hand in the bra to caress her breasts, her eyes were wide in exclamation.

'Pradeep,' she squeaked and got hold of her hand and suddenly bra gave way exposing her bosom.

She thrusted Pradeep and squeaked, 'Pradeep I am orthodox, no such activity before marriage. Get out from here and get the packed dinner for tonight.'

Pradeep grinned went out to take packed dinner, and returned in no time.

When he asked Vibha to take dinner she told that she was not famishing.

Pradeep cajoled her and requested her to take dinner, but vibha was in no mood to relent.

'Vibha please, he took her face in between both palms and said,' Vibha I am sorry.'

Suddenly she broke down and embraced him, 'Pradeep you should not have done so, saw my nude body, I am still feeling ashamed of.'

'Vibha I did not see you, just glimpses of your boobs.'

'Pradeep,' she whimpered, 'don't tell.'

He groaned.

When he returned to his apartment there was a call from Neelima, 'Pradeep where are you, I am missing you a lot.'

'Neelima I also miss you a lot.'

'Then why did you not call me since you had gone from Delhi. Three days had passed, you did not make any call.'

'Neelima, I thought you must be angry after the episode in night, when I did not perform sex, and you were really annoyed. You did not spoke much in morning when you came to station to drop me. Neelima what should I do, I have been taught so from my childhood—sex after marriage.'

'Pradeep it had impressed me, you are dfferent person. Had there have been another man in your place he would have insisted for physical contact and never have lost such an opportunity to perform sexual act with the girl who had sexual appeal, a model and attractive. But you controlled yourself, which made me determined to marry you. Now tell me when are you coming? I am missing you my sweet heart.'

'On Sunday.'

'Sunday,' she squeaked. 'Come on Saturday,' she whimpered, 'Please Pradeep, come on Saturday and we would decide the date for marriage so that you don't have any immorality attached to look at my boobs,' she giggled.

Pradeep agreed to go to Delhi on Saturday after persistent requests from Neelima.

He would be the best husband on earth, wont seduce other women and I would enjoy sex with you as well as other folks also, Neelima was thinking.

Pradeep understood what was in her mind. He would be her husband and stick to her, but she would be free to have her valley dampened by the water sprinkled by other folks. He would have to stroll on damp grass in the valley while he would be her master but stroll on slippery valley, Pradeep was lost in thoughts. He would never marry her. At the same time her prodding protuberances flashed infront of him, and he developed sudden urge to make her wet by her masculine organ, what was immoral in this, both were adults and wanted to enjoys physical union, This time on Saturday night, he would make her wet deep inside, for the first time in life, though she had been made wet by many guests beforeore, it was adorned by many frequent visitors . . .

Pradeep got up early in the morning and walked to balcony to peer out. Students were going to college for the first class. And suddeny he sighted the magnificent posterior protrusions, 'Oh Maitreyi!' He spelled and clinged her eyes to her bobbling protrusions when his organ was becoming fuller with increased inflow of the blood.

In the hospital when Vibha came he told her that he was going to Delhi on Saturday.

'Why?' she squeaked.

'Vibha I have done operations whose dressing is my duty, after this visit I will tell Neelima that he will not be able to come to Delhi.' It pacified Vibha and she smiled placidly. 'Now you can call your father and fix the date of marriage.' Vibha was rejoicing the moments, which were her cherished desire, if that is so let him go on Saturday.

On Saturday, I will ravish you Neelima, if so many people have wandered in your valley, I should also get an opportunity to visit, and forget marriage; I will love to enjoy unadorned valley rather then frequently visited place for permanent relationship, called marriage. I otherwise also don't love the crowd and long to visit the places uninhabited, Neelima, yes once I shall visit and forget everything, forget marriage.

Vibha made a call to his father who told that he could come the next Sunday, Pradeep agreed to meet father.

Vibha went away when Maitreyi sneaked into the chamber, her evections were even more maddening than those of Neelima.

'Sir, I have told my parents that how you had saved me from falling, they wanted to meet you sir,' she said her lips moving and sending innumerable waves inside him.

'Sir you would go to Delhi this Sunday?'

'This weekend, I shall go on Saturday,' he told.

'Sir, I shall also go on Saturday and my father has requested you to stay with us,' she requested.

Pradeep was noncommittal, after sometime he told that he would stay with one of the aquaintances.

'So on Sunday stay with us, sir, we would come together on Monday.'

'I shall keep your proposal in mind, but cant assure any thing as of now.'

'No problem, sir.'

She was stunning beauty, better than Neelima and unblemished adorned, whar her parents wanted to day, marriage, not sure . . .

In the evening pradeep went to the apartment of Vibha and took the chairs to the balcony, Vibha was bubbling, 'Pradeep I love you, scared of somebody snatching you from me,' said she and rested her head against the his shoulders, he took her face between the palms and put his lips over hers when Vibha felt rush of blood to her valley which became moist.

'Oh Pradeep!' She let herself go loose in his arms, he put his lips down over her neck and lower further.

Why she had become so loose, unable to resist, let him do what he wanted to do, he was his man afterall.

Vibha encircled her arm around him, Pradeep reached to her hips, searching her body for some thing to read that, lips taking the rounded firmer flesh knob at the evections on her bosom and Vibha was in a frenzied attack of sexual excitement. She was burning inside with desire, desire to be engulfed, desire to be rattled by some one and desire to feel the engorged flesh of his man, but as soon as his hand reached at the tuft of hair and the small flesh of ecstacy beneath, she disdainfully drifted,' Pradeep, after marriage.

Pradeep went to Delhi with Maitreyi on Saturday evening. Neelima had arrived to receive him. Maitreyi requested Pradeep to come to her house to which Neelima said that at this hour they were late, if Pradeep wanted, he would come the next day. Maitreyi agreed and told that she would come to take him. Neelima was envious of her, she had to treasure Pradeep, otherwise some other girl would take him over. He was man, broad shoulders, handsome and plastic surgeon; who would not like him to insert his throbbing engorged flesh inside their valleys. She would also go with Pradeep, she was determined.

At home Pradeep went upstairs, tidied himself and came down for dinner. Father of Neelima along with mother also accompanied him for dinner.

'My son, think of marriage,' she said, 'Neelima talks so much of you, loves you so much, both of you should go for marriage soon,' mother suggested.

Pradeep agreed.

After dinner Pradeep came to his room and lay on bed, her moher was much interested in marriage, but how could he marry her, she would have extramarital relations while he would wait for her at home. But her body was sensuous, just her presence made him mad for her, she should have come, he was missing her, wished to ravish her, so hard that she would remember only one man, Pradeep.

She came and without waiting for any formalities hugged,' Hi, Pradeep I miss you so much, now plan to come to Delhi permanently,' she said and put her lips over his, sucked them and darted her lip inside the mouth.

'Pradeep I miss you a lot,' she said and pulling his hand brought him outside in open sky.' Pradeep look at sky,' she said clutching his hand and caressing his strong and powerful fingers.

'Who is this girl?'

'Maitreyi? She is student.'

'I am scared of so many women surrounding you.'

Pradeep grinned, 'Why?'

'Oh, I am scared as some of the girl might entice you and you might forget Neelima.

'Oh Neelima!' he kept her arms around her and put his head over her boobs, moving his head side to side slowly and soflty, put his index finger over her lips, exploring the sensuality.

Neelima was already aroused, by the actions Pradeep was doing she was immensely aroused and she felt pulations inside her body, and severe ignition and boiling fluid flowing inside her body.

'Neelima I also miss you a lot, and want to marry you soon.' In heart he was thinking Neelima he would never marry a woman like her so adorned by many visitors, but he wished to visit her valley once, might be that night.

'Pradeep shift to Delhi, so many patients are there, marry me.' She was thinking that she would have a husband who was plain and idiot in matters of sex, shrouded by the wrap of morality, he would never touch another woman, the biggest advantgae, what she wanted in her husband.

Every man and woman want their partners to be simple and committed to them only, while they want to wander around to many guests, same was true for Neelima too.

After some time maid brought the tray with two mugs of coffee, Neelima might have told her already. She put the tray on the parapet and went away. Neelima lifted one cup and gave it to Pradeep.

'Why two mugs?' Pradeep asked.

'One would do, but till we are married, to the other members of the house we have to show that we are two and not one, which we would be after marriage.'

Pradeep grinned and took a sip from the mug, Neelima lifted her cup to sip. The moon was round and large, full moon as it is called and glittering light and rays were coming to her face and boobs, and they were also glittering. She was superb in that light.

They kept on sitting over there for some time, kissing, and fondling her boobs, when his hand descended further over the tuft of hair to search for the flesh just beneath, the flesh of feminism, she writhed, 'Pradeep don't do don't do . . . I am aroused and then you run away with out quenching my thirst. I just cry the whole night.'

'Neelima,' he said and guided her hand over his pulsating flesh engorged with persistent sensuality. 'Ah!' Neelima writhed with mirth and got hold of his hand, pulled him in the room.

'Pradeep don't run away this time, no moral preachings, and any way you are my man now, it is only rituals which are to be compelted.'

Who was interested in rituals, Pradeep thought. He would ravish you, deeply thoroughly and in entirety. No marriage. You say that marriage is not requirement for sex, he has also started believing in it.

Neelima thrusted him in the room and just tore open his trousers and shirts, she was just enraged with flowing of blood, at fast pace . . . and clutched to hold his pulsating flesh . . .

She shown her pulsating flesh covering the valley and put his hand to rub that fiercely and put his flesh in between and suddenly clutched his posterior. 'Thrust Pradeep, today You cant runaway, and as he was about to insert, somebody knocked at the door, Neelima immediately cluctched his posteriors and thrusted him inside her, 'Ah!' She yelled, 'Pradeep break me in pieces, thrust so deeply that I wince with pain of enjoyment and there were thrusts, longing for each others lips, boobs and suddenly every thing became wet soothingly wet, pleasurable wet, the weteness of lust, wetness of love and wetness of sexual enjoyment . . ."

Next day Pradeep went with Neelima to Grover nursing home, Patients for dressing had already come, Pradeep asked the nurse to take them to dressing room one by one, she told two new patients had also come, Pradeep told that he would see after the dressing. First patient of mammoplasty was perfectly normal, she was doing massage as was told. There was no problem, so Pradeep told that after one week she could go braless, if she so desired. Mrs Dwivedi was next patient, her dressing was changed and she was told to massage with flat of palm which was to reduce the capsular contracture, Pradeep told her.

After dressings he examined two patients—one was for mammoplasty and another was for finger contracture, Pradeep posted both patients for operation on next Sunday. 'Maitreyi was coming to pick him up', Pradeep told Neelima.

'I will accompany you.'

'Why?'

'You dont know, I miss you so much and scared too.'

Pradeep laughed, 'OK.'

She would not leave him, Pradeep thought, while Neelima was thinking that she was not going to leave him. He had enjoyed sex with her, he had to pay the price for it in the form of marriage, he had to forget other women.

Maitreyi came to pick them up from hospital, she came out of driver's seat and opened the side door for Pradeep. But Neelima was too fast, she opened the rear door for Pradeep and sat herself beside Maitreyi.

She was not his assistant Vibha who would sit behind, Neelima would sit in front and by the side of the girl, whom he might kiss as he kissed her. When he had sex with her, he could not have relations with anyother, that was his morality preached him.

Neelima was too fast Pradeep was thinking, must be scared that he might kiss Maitreyi also as he had kissed her, Vibha was too innocent she sat on rear seat without rasing any objections. Maitreyi parked the car infront of her hosue which was no less magnificient than that of Neelima's. She opened the gate and stood aside for both of them to enter the house. She introduced Pradeep to his father, 'Dad he is my sir Pradeep sir, Plastic surgeon he saved me from falling,' Dad shook his hand, 'Our family is greatful to you my son. Come have a seat, he offered a seat to him.

Pradeep sat on sofa alongwith Neelima. Dad was curious to know the introduction of the woman with him.

'She is Neelima—actress.'

'Oh yes, I was thinking that she must be Neelima.'

'She is my patient and helping me in settling in Delhi, 'Pradeep told but father was not much convinced, she was his patient, but why did she wander with him. There was something going on between two.

Father was not convinced, Pradeep thought, being patient one did not room around.

After exchange of pleasantries and light breakfast Pradeep came out with Neelima, Maitreyi dropped them at Grover nursing home where her car was parked.

Neelima started the car and opened the door for Pradeep, who sat beside her. 'You were very much interested in sitting beside her,' Neelima quipped. Pradeep grinned and said, 'You were smart enough to sit beside her.'

'Pradeep!' she quipped, 'Now you wont look at any other woman except me. If you are so eager to caress my thighs, kiss them. But all the males are alike, you are also no different. No eagerness to kiss my thinghs now but of Miatreyi's. All men behave like this, once they stroll inside the feminine valley, they lose all interest in the stroll at valley again.'

Pradeep grinned, she was right, for the first time he was not deveoping an urge to caress or kiss at her thighs or caress her boobs.

Neelima stopped the car in front of her house and did not come out of the car. 'Now what is plan?' she enquired. 'I shall go in evening.'

'Why to go in evening. Stay overnight, in the morning go to Aligarh and start binding up the things in Aligarh, it is no place for you,' she suggested. He was in dilemma, developing an urge to indulge in dalliance again in the night, but Vibha would kill him. She had phoned so many times since morning, and every time asking him to return by the night. She had also asked him not to take any new cases further.

This dilemma always harassed him, though in morning he was not much sensually aroused, but again he developed an urge to have stroll in her garden.

'Neelima I should go in the evening,' he said just to know her reaction, though he was not interested in going.

She quipped, 'You are not going in the evening but in morning, understood.' Pradeep grinned.

After lunch Pradeep went upstairs and lay on bed. Maitreyi was superb sensuous, more than Neelima, radiating warmth of youthful skin, the sensuality radiating from her body had lanced him all over. But he should not think in carnal way, she was his student. He should not be so immoral. Where all preachings had banished. He had enjoyed the **valley stroll** before marriage, and eyeing Maitreyi.

When Maitreyi reached home her parents were waiting for her. 'Dropped at home?'

'Not at the home dad, her car was parked at Grover Nursing home so I dropped them over there.'

'Ok,' they agreed, 'Doctor is nice, is he unmarried?'

'Yes, but why are you asking mom?'

'For you.'

'For myself?'

'Yes, you are grown up and he would prove a good husband for you.'

'Husband, mom don't start thinking so soon.'

'But there is no harm in thinking and exploring the possibilities'.

'Oh mom,' she blushed.

'Find out more about him, any relations with other woman, particularly this woman—Neelima.'

'Mom how can I find any thing like that from him, he is my teacher.'

'No problem, we would come to Aligarh, meet him and ask directly.'

Maitreyi looked at mom and her eagerness to marry her as soon as she gets good man.

There was nothing wrong if Pradeep marries to her, she had not thought before, he was famous plastic surgeon and heart throb of so many girls.

Pradeep was lost in Maitreyi, why their parents had called him to the house, her daughter was grown up and they might be exploring the possibility of marriage, Neelima was also scared because of that. She wanted to marry him for one simple reason, he would not go to any other *woman and she would go to any other man. Foolish lady. Even if she had gone to many men, after marriage she would not be able to frequent, and he was strict for that.*

Vibha phoned him that he should not stay back in Delhi. Pradeep said, 'Vibha I have to the dressing of mammoplasty patient, she had infection, so I had done dressing in the morning and had do it again in the evening, I would come in the morning.'

'Pradeep,' she quipped, 'Are you telling the truth or that witch has enticed you again. From now onwards I wont allow you to walk again like that.'

There was no doubt that Neelima had enticed him, and at the same time she came, clad in short skirt flanked by blue shirt which was also short from above, showing the sensous skin of her boobs.

'Looking superb,' he spelled, feeling sudden rush to caress the naked beauty of her boobs.

'Come out side, we have asked maid to bring tea and some eatables, its very pleasant over here.' Pradeep got to his toes and straightening the wrinkles from over kurta and trousers, he walked outside.

The weather was really pleasant, he pulled out a chair and sat, Neelima sat on other chair, and lifted a cup to give to Pradeep, and held another cup for herself.

'Pradeep what are you planning now for shifting?'

'How can I shift so soon, I have to search for a nice accommodation.'

'Accomodation!What are you speaking, such big house and all vacant rooms, you still need to search for accommodation?'

'How can I stay in this house for long?'

'This house is of yours, Neelima's and you should not search for accommodation. Shift in this house.'

'Neelima . . .'

'No further discussion, next week you are shifting to Delhi.'

'Neelima, I have to give three months 'notice, only then I can shift.'

'Three months! 'she squeaked, no way, I cant wait for three months, I love you so much and miss you so much. I wish to marry you so that I get a body guard, a man who is mine.'

He should marry her so that she could invite others for stroll, Pradeep was thinking.

The evening was pleasant and soon the night descended to meet his woman and at the same time Neelima clutched his hand and said, 'Would you like to go anywhere?'

'Where?'

'Disco.'

'Disco.'

'No not all,' Pradeep was bewildered. 'I don't like to frequent such places.'

'No problem, just watch TV, I am to discuss the plot of a new serial, would return in one hour.'

'I will wait, but come soon,' Pradeep requested.

I know where are you going and for what!

You are fool, you should have demanded yourself to go with me, who was going to discuss the scene . . . You are so innocent that in todays era you are unfit . . .

Must be thinking that he was a fool, he knew everything where she was going and for what, but why should he insisit to go with her, he was not marrying to her any way.

Neelima went to Hemant house where she wanted to discuss the story for new movie, Hemant was the well known producer of many films and was much inclined to Neelima.

'Neelima, how are you?' he shook her hand.

She giggled. 'I am alright.'

'What will you take? Rum or gin? ?'

'Gin would do.'

'Yes, he went inside the house and brought two pegs, one for himself and other for Neelima. Maid came and served the salted cashews. Neelima took a sip and lifted one cashew to nibble at.

'This is the drink, you ask Pradeep he would say either tea or coffee,' she grinned.

'What happend?' Hemant asked.

'Nothing, I was just thinking of a doctor, Pradeep.'

'You told me that he was a plastic surgeon.'

'Right.'

'He is here, in Delhi?'

'Yes, he had done two superb mammoplasties.'

'Neelima, get my wife's boobs also corrected.'

'Why?'

'Her boobs are too loose, get them tightened.'

'I don't know it can also be done or not, ok let me ask doctor.' She called Pradeep to ask whether loose boobs can be made tighter or not?'

Pradeep answered that loose boobs could be made tighter and larger.

Neelima told, 'Hemant my doctor is saying that boobs can be made tighter and larger too,' she told and winked at her.

'When?'

'Next Sunday.'

'Ok, you get everything arranged and get it done on Sunday.'

'Let me ask,' said Neelima and again called Pradeep. 'Pradeep can you do it next Sunday?'

'Yes.'

'You will like to examine before operation?'

'I may examine on Sunday just before operation.'

'Done Hemant,' she assured Hemant when he pulled her over his lap and kissed her, 'Hey! you are talking so much about the doctor, are you involved with him?'

'Nothing like that.'

'Otherwise I will just murder him.'

'Hemant I am not involved, but need a man to be called a husband, he is fitting in that category', she giggled and laughed.

'So got hold of a fool?' he said and burst in laughter.

'Yes,' she giggled again.

She returned home at about 10 pm, parents were waiting for dinner. 'Neelima doctor is in house, what would he think.' Mother was not in good mood. 'You are grown up, should come to home early, we are thinking for marriage and at least in his presence she should act in sombre way.'

Neelima grinned.

'Call him for dinner, must be famishing,' mother told her to call Pradeep.

He came down with Neelima who had gone to call him.

'My son, take care of her, she is not controllable. Returned at 10, a girl of good family does not remain out side home till 10 pm, only you can control her.'

'Yes mom,' Pradeep said. He did not like Neelima going out for so long. Her mother was very much intersted in marriage while she was of differnt type, he did not speak much.

'Son is angry with you Neelima, you should not have gone leaving him alone,' mother commented.

'No mom, nothing like that, I was just feeling sleepy,' Pradeep said.

After dinner he came up. Neelima told not to sleep, she was coming with milk, or coffee, what did he like?

'Coffee.'

'Ok,' she agreed.

After sometime she went up to the room of Pradeep. 'Neelima mother is not happy.'

'Yes, I know.'

'Why have you come so late?'

'Where it is late doctor, ten in night is not late,' Neelima argued.

'I think it is late,' Pradeep persisted.

'Oh doctor come on,' she clutched his hand and put over her lips, 'You marry me, and I would not go out of home.'

She would go out of home and would return at 10, he knew, and so he would not marry her, Pradeep thought.

He was not feeling sensuality of her body her lips and and her boobs. What had happened, he was amused. As he had taken a stroll at her garden, sensuality had vanished or what.

Neelima was caressing his fingers with her lips and then she put his hand over her boobs. Today he was cool. Neelima noticed. Doctor I know how to make man hot. Marry me and every thing would be alright, you are showing me your behaviour, and then I will show mine. She thought and put his hand inside the bra over boobs and Pradeep who was feeling unaroused, suddenly felt some blood rushing to his flesh.

He moved his fingers over the boobs and clutched hold the tiny fleshy knob over the peak of ecstatic boobs.

And flow of blood rushed to have his organ throb.

'Doctor Kiss me, ravish me, I cant remain without you, Come, go deep inside.'

Next morning Neelima dropped him at station and warned him that if he did not start shifting, she would come to Aligarh and get all luggage shifted, Pradeep grinned.

Train moved when Pradeep entered. Maitreyi was already there in the compartment. He walked to her and sat beside her. 'Father was praising you a lot,' she told.

'Why, what is there to praise?'

'You are a great plastic surgeon, good human being and most important you have saved me from falling.'

He grinned.

'Sir may I ask you something?'

'Ask.'

'Sir, why have you not done marriage?'

'Marriage!' he smiled, 'Did not get a good girl.'

'What type of girl you are looking for sir?'

'Like you,' he said hurriedly, she blushed.

To continue the conversation he asked, 'Are you the only child of your parents?'

'Yes sir.'

'My parents are very much interested in you.'

He smiled.

At station they got down and Pradeep went to hospital straight and opened his chamber when registrar came, 'Sir you will like to take the round first or go for operations. "What are the cases?' he enquired.

'Sir, there are three cases—abdominoplasty, vaginoplasty and tuboplasty.'

'All difficult cases, I will like to do abdominoplasty first.'

'Alright sir,' registrar said and went to operation room to get the patient of abdominoplasty shifted.

Vibha entered. 'Whenever you go to Delhi always stay back for extended day, that witch has really enticed you,' she commented.

'Its not like that Vibha, I had told you that I had to do dressing of the patient in the evening.'

'Hey don't tell me a lie,' she retorted.

'How?'

'You have not done dressing in evening.'

'How can you say that?'

'I have phoned them and asked, and they told me you had not gone there in the evening.'

Pradeep was taken aback and thought it was right not to argue further.

'Now you wont go to Delhi or I will go with you,' Vibha told him sternly.

He just looked at her.

'She has enticed you, whenever you go to Delhi, kiss her on thighs, on her boohs, or else do something nasty. All the men are same, got a beautiful woman and become mad. But it is not expected from Pradeep, he was different.'

'Ah I have not kissed any where Vibha,' he got up and took her in his arms, lowering his face gave her a kiss.

My Vibha is there for kissing, why should I kiss somebody else.

Oh, you can kiss at her thighs in my presence, so don't petend as if you are very disciplined man.'

'Forget that one incidence Vibha.'

'How can I forget that one incidence, when I saw my man kissing somebody else at her thighs at her boobs, I was burning inside I should have slapped you with my pointed heel sandals. Alas! I could not do that.'

Pradeep laughed.

'Hey don't laugh, you have not done some heroic act but mean act, how can somebody even think of some other woman in presence of her own woman; too mean and disgusting.'

Pradeep became serious and gloomy. 'Vibha those were bad moments, I also don't know how did it happen, so sorry for that.'

If you had been sorry then you would not have met her, but you ferquented her, stayed with her, how could I believe that you were not doing some filty activities, not kissing her boobs, I believed you must be doing all such activities. She would make you to do that, her dress, so provocative that any onlooker would have developed an urge to caress her thigs or boobs, her dress never covered . . .'

'Oh, you also had an urge to caress,' Pradeep commented.

'Not me, why should I develop urge to caress her boobs, **poor men did that who are the fools before beautiful women's naked body, just fools,** and I am sorry to say my man also become a fool.'

'Vibha,' he separated from her, 'You may say what you wish because I am your culprit, standing before you.' Vibha was about to say some thing when registrar knockd at the door and came inside. He informed that patient had been shifted to operation room.

Pradeep sat on chair to open the shoe strings and change to OT shoes, Vibha walked out to take her own round, once at the gate, she warned, 'Now you are not going to Delhi at all.'

Pradeep nodded in agreement with what she said.

She was ordering as if she was my wife, till marriage, you could not prevent me. And how could he forget Neelima, so ecstatic, the woman who had given him the pleasure of physical union, for the first time in life, how could heforget her boobs and her posterior protuberances and every bit of her body. He could not forget. She would be my friend, and he would have the opportunity to suck at her boobs so sensuous, mere thinking about her body made the blood inside his body to rush at fast pace. But he would not marry her at all. And Maitreyi . . . . , her parents, most probabaly were interested in marrying her to him. She was good no doubt, younger and passionate, before he had seen her as student in white apron but when he saw her in jeans and shirt, she was superbly sensuous and passionate than Neelima, her skin was more glowing than that of Neelima and perhaps she was not having guests visiting to her ecstatic valley.

In that case he would prefer Maitreyi over others. Ecstatic, and beautiful, unadorned; celibate beauty, she was.

Soon he put on the sterile dress and went to the operation room, the patient was shifted and anesthetized, he ordered registrar to scrub the abdomen and catheterize the patient.

After operation he came to his chamber when Maitreyi came.

'Sir may I come in.'

He looked at the door, Maitreyi was standing over there.'

'Come Maitreyi.'

She walked inside the chamber, wearing an apron under which was hidden her beauty, beautifully carved out protuberances and glistening skin of the naked abdomen; but her protrusions were still ecstatic through apron. Pradeep was ogling at her, she blushed, he was going to be her man, she thought and smiled; my parents would get him for her.

'Sir, I do not understand hernia, please teach me and clear my doubts.'

'Maitreyi at present I cant explain you but you may come to my apartment in the evening.'

At the same time Vibha entered, Pradeep became jittery, Maiteryi, finding Vibha in, walked out of the chamber.

'Why have you called her to apartment?' She was suscipicious. Pradeep could know by the lines on her face that she had become envious.

'Vibha don't be suscipcious of every girl, she had come to learn something, so I called her at apartment.

'College has no space to teach so you called her at apartment!' she passed sarcastic remark, 'Pradeep, I am sorry to say, you are becoming womanizer.'

'Nothing like that Vibha,' he tried to explain, 'Her parents has asked me to take her care.'

'Her parents? Where did you meet them? ?'

'This Sunday.'

'Where?'

'Maitreyi had taken me to her house.'

'Ah!now Maitreyi is also to be envious of. You didn't have time to meet my father, but had time to go to other's house also, and tell me a lie, that patient had to be dressed, Pradeep . . . Pradeep . . . ,' Vibha was squeaking. 'I will also come in evening, you are not at all trust worthy,' she told firmly and walked out of chamber.

She was always after him, let him enjoy and feel sensuality of beautiful women, their naked bodies, boobs, thighs, and feminine flesh, once married, every thing would be past . . .

As Vibha went away, he got a call from Neelima, 'How are you Pradeep I am missing you a lot, please shift to Delhi, I cant live without you.'

'I am also missing you Neelima, today I might submit resignation and start shifting, it would take three months.'

'Three months,' she squeaked, 'I will die in three months, your Neelima would die in three months, Pradeep'.

His Neelima, Pradeep was thinking, she was liar, she must be Neelima of so many, she was not his Neelima exclusively, she just wanted to marry him for society so that she might wander any where and allowed as many guests to visit her sensuous valley, but he was not moron.'

'Pradeep are you listening?'

'Yes, I am listening Neelima,' Pradeep said softly.

'I am missing you Pradeep, come tomorrow.'

'Tomorrow!It will not be possible to come tomorrow, I have to operate patient over here,' Pradeep reasoned.

'In that case come on Friday.'

'Neelima try to understand I cant come.'

'Why, why cant you come on Friday?' Neelima put up a question sternly.

'Neelima,' he was soft.

'Come on Friday,' she retorted.

'Ok, I will come on Saturday, if everything is alright,' Pradeep told her.

'Come, Pradeep we would talk of marriage,' Neelima explained.

'Marriage or no marriage, I am coming on Saturday,' he assured Neelima.

'That's like good man.'

After her call, Pradeep was baffled, if he informed Vibha that he would be going on Saturday to Delhi, she would throttle him, but her sensuous touch, kisses and the stroll he had taken in the ecstatic garden and then in the valley, aroused him passionately and he developed an urge to run to her grove and exstatic dale again and how he would wait till Saturday, he would go on Friday and would tell Vibha that he was going to Agra as his mother was not feeling well, he smiled on the plot he created to deceive Vibha.

In the evening Maitreyi came, she removed the apron she was wearing and her beauty was ajar, her short blue shirt was more maddening than of Neelima's and so was white shorts through which her glistening white skin of legs was visibly maddening. Neelima's boobs were also bigger but not so protuberant, he developed an urge to kiss at them, but he resisted, she was your student, Neelima was your friend; whatever it might be, blood inside his body was rushing at fast pace.

'Yes, Maitreyi what you wish to ask?'

'Sir, I am not able to understand the difference between direct and indirect hernia.'

Pradeep got the right opportunity to touch her feminine beauty, 'Inguinal hernia comes out of inguinal rings which are situated just by the side of the bush of sexual hair and feminine flesh knob, which arouse any man intensively. He would caress and make her passionately aroused, may be she started or said something. He could advance to her primarily, woman would not advance, lead has to be taken by him, let him see.

He said, 'Maitreyi both come out of inguinal rings, but only indirect comes through deep inguinal ring. You understand where the superficial ring is situated?' he asked.

'No.'

'Come near to me, I shall tell you.'

Maitreyi came nearer to him when he was about to pull her skirt up a bit and see the bush of the hair and perhaps go lower down, which was maddening him and Maitreyi was seducing him. She understood what he was thinking, but she had come for that purpose, but touch only, no further.

As he was lifting her skirt a bit, somebody knocked at the gate.

Vibha you are after me, Pradeep knew she would be at the gate.

He got up to open the door. Maitreyi put on the apron she had removed.

Pradeep thought if Vibha would see Maitreyi in skimpy clothes she would beat him as well her.

Scared of Vibha he opened the door and welcomed her to come inside. When they came to drawing hall, Pradeep took a sigh of relief when he saw Maitreyi having put on apron in which all her naked flesh was hidden and well protected.

'Its intelligent move,' Pradeep thought.

Vibha cast a searching glance over Maiteryi and found her short skirt too objectionable, 'Maitreyi it is your dress particularly when you have come to sir's apartment.'

'I am so sorry madam.'

'Maitreyi you did not get time in college, so you had to come over here in sir's apartment, 'she asked sternly.

Maitreyi did not say a word.

'Vibha she is a girl student, why are you thinking in carnal way,' Pradeep tried to pacify her.

'Pradeep,' she retorted,' All girls are innocent like Neelima, you have touched and kissed her thighs, her boobs, she was a simple Neelima, and now kiss her thighs also and say she is simple student, **all men are alike, dogs drooling saliva once they saw women bodies, why did you allow her if she was not in proper dress, because you relished her body, you have become womanizer, want to kiss her thighs, her boobs . . .**

'Vibha what are you saying about her?'

'Keep silent,' Vibha retrorted and then turning to Maitreyi she squeaked, 'Get out from here and never come in this dress again.'

'Ok madam,' Maiteyi gathered her notebook and rose to her toes to rush back.

'Maitreyi,' Pradeep called her.

'Pradeep she would go back and come in proper clothes,' she intervened.

Maitreyi opened the door and went out.

This madam is very mean, always think of wrong things, why she was so much enraged; she is not his wife, had spoiled the mood of sir also, poor Pradeep sir, could not speak a word in front of her. She must have taken few steps only when she got a call from her father, who wanted to talk to Pradeep as Maitreyi had told him that she would be going in the evening to Pradeep sir's apartment for study. She returned back and knocked at the door, Pradeep opened the door and finding Maitreyi over there was baffled, but Maitreyi immediately said, 'Sir phone call from my father for you.'

Pradeep looked at Vibha and took the phone from her.

'Hi Pradeep, just called to know your father's phone no.'

Pradeep looked at Vibha through the corners of his eyes, she was looking at Pradeep, he became nervous, she had just made me her doggy.

'I will sms you sir.'

'Ok and hope every thing is alright I suppose.'

'Yes sir.'

Pradeep disconnected the phone and handed over to Maitreyi when his fingers touched her' s, he kept on holding the fingers for sometime, when Vibha moved to them, 'What's matter?' She found Pradeep holding her hand.

'What's the matter?' she squeaked, 'You are still here.'

'Madam there was a phone call from my father who wanted to talk to Pradeep sir.' She was also strict this time, holding the phone she turned to go out. 'Vibha sometimes you overreact, she is a student.'

I know all girl students, all girls and women are alike, as all men are alike like you, and you were holding her hand, why for what reasons? A teacher is supposed to hold the hand of his student, and caress her fingers and perhaps lips and boobs and perhaps lower down. All the men are alike.'

Why the madam was so much angry, Maitreyi was puzzled, her dress was normal, skirt which girls wear, shirt, which girls wear, what was wrong with her dress. Might be she was in love with Pradeep sir. If that is so, she would take it as a challenge—challenge to grab Pradeep sir and snatch from her clutches. The way she was retorting at Pradeep sir, she was puzzled, should have slapped her if she would not have been teacher at college, it was no way to insult and that to in other's apartment.

When Vibha went away Pradeep was lost in day's incidences, he was puzzled why Vibha was so furious. She was not his wife, no body knew what was going to happen, if a young girl had come in that dress why to find the faults with dress. Imagination of her skirts made him flurried, passion rising inside and flowing at fast pace alover his body, his parts becoming engorged with rapid flow of blood. And not only skirt if she had seen her without apron she would have become mad. Her protuberancs were maddening . . .

Why Pradeep behaved in this manner in the matter of women, Vibha was puzzled, he should not have called the student at her apartment, and she had come in skimpy dress, he should have told her to come in proper dress; he did not do that rather he was clutching his hand too, was he same Pradeep to whom she loved. He kissed over her thighs, her boobs, she had seen him doing that and today he was holding her fingers; he was changed, If his behaviour in matter of women continued like that, she had to think twice before marrying him. Why he was after women, she was there, but he had not done with her, but Vibha she had not allowed him to do anything always, resisted his moves.

Yes, she would allow all that after marriage not before, she was strict. If he was changed man, she would not hang for him—whether marriage materialized or not.

Pradeep opened the chamber when registrar came for the round. At the same time Maitreyi also came. Pradeep asked the registrar to start the round, he would join. He turned to maitreyi. 'I am sorry Maitreyi for her beahviour,' Pradeep said.

'Its alright sir, why she was so angry, I am not able to understand, what was wrong with my dress.'

'Maitreyi she is woman of old values.'

'Even then sir there was no need to be so much angry. She should not have misbehaved not only with me but you also sir ', she said.

Enshrouding her body with apron, she was appearing sombre but beneath that lay the passionate body. 'Sir when should I come for study? I shall come over here and not to your apartment.'

'Come at 1 pm,' Pradeep called her at one in afternoon and developed an urge to feel her inguinal ring, or passionate small bud of sensuous flesh. Vibha would have gone by that time for lunch.

Maitreyi nodded and went away.

Pradeep rose to his feet and walked to the ward. Vibha should not have misbehaved in that way, no doubt, she had no right to criticise her dress. What is a woman if hidden in clothes, Pradeep was lost in thoughts, but to expose one sould have the beautiful body. Which was not the case with Vibha, what was there in Vibha, no prodding boobs, no the shapely thighs, even if she appears in skirt, short skirt, she would appear ugly rather than sensuous or sexy.

In the ward patient of abdominoplasty was alright, her drain from the abdomen was to be removed, so he asked the registrar to shift the patient to the dressing room. Other patients were alright and did not require dressing. Registrar asked the nurse to shift the patient to the dressing room, Pradeep asked nurse to remove the dressing and bring scisors and forceps to cut stitches to remove the drain which was put to drain the collection of blood if any. After drain was removed, he told the patient you had got the flat abdomen. Patient was happy. She was having lower abdominal bulges which not only looked unsightly but interfered in sex also. 'When I can resume the sexual activity?' she enquired.

'May be after three weeks,' he suggested, not before.

'Three weeks!How can one remain for 3 weeks with out sex?'

Pradeep was stunned at her response, perhaps nonmedico are bolder than doctors themselves, he thought.

When he returned to chamber Vibha came. She was not in happy mood, 'Pradeep you are changed now.'

'How you can say that?'

'You are womanizer now, Neelima and now this Maitreyi; what had happened to you?'

Pradeep glanced at her, 'Womanizer.'

'Yes womanizer, I was shocked to see you clutching her hand.'

'Vibha it is not like that.'

'Its like that Pradeep, both incidences took place in front of my eyes, many more must have happened behind me; who knew you might have kissed at her thighs also, thighs of Maitreyi or at boobs or at her . . . her . . .'

'What her?'

'At her sexual parts,' she said hurriedly.

'Vibha what are you saying?'

'I am saying what I feel must be true, if you could clutch her hand in front of me, you could have kissed at her genitals too, same is true for Neelima's body too. You have kissed her thighs and boobs in my presence, then who would have prevented you to kiss at her genitals, and who knew you might have gone further and pierced her virginity . . .'

Pradeep was silent. She was right, he had taken a stroll at her garden and that was the lovely moment of his life, the garden, the valley, the earth wettened by him, sprinkled by him, watered by him; so sensuous, so pleasurable and he had done that for the first time in life, while Vibha never let him touch her boobs what to say of stroll in cave, in valley. Ok such activities after marriage, but its not law, both adults could have enjoyment if they agreed.

'Pradeep where are you? Lost in Neelima or Maitreyi?'

'No, Vibha, I have to Agra on Friday.'

'Why?'

'Mother is missing me.'

'Mother or Neelima at Delhi,' Vibha casted sarcastic remark.

'Vibha why are so sarcastic?'

'Because your behaviour is like that, you are a changed man now.'

Pradeep again looked at her. Yes he was a changed man, he was actual man now had taken stroll at her valley, for the first time, he had to be changed man; the man who had tasted the fruits of forbidden valley, sensuous valley, had to be chaged man and suddenly he developed longing to be with Neelima to caress her thighs, her boobs and her tiny flesh along with the flesh on either side of the entrance to ecsatic valley. so sensuous, so pleasurable indeed.

'If mother wants to meet, do go, my best wishes for her.'

Pradeep gave a wide grin.

Maitreyi came at 1 pm while Vibha had gone for lunch.

'So Maitreyi you want to know the inguinal ring?' Asked Pradeep.

'Yes sir.'

That would be better depicted in skirt, today she was wearing the jeans and in that it would be difficult to explain.

Pradeep, you are womanizer, Vibha was right he should not have done so with Maitreyi, but he could not stop himself and asked her to come nearer. See, it is pubic tubercle he lowered her jeans and leered at, the bush of hair where pubic tubercle was visible and he developed urge to caress that, but he maintained serious attitude and told her that it was pubic tubercle.

Sir, now Vibha would be taught a lesson, I am a Delhite girl and now you would be after me.

She clucthed his hand and put over her hair and down.

Pardeep was taken aback by her open attitude and he immediately put her lips over hers, kissing her.

She did not leave his hand and massaged her flesh, small knob of flesh and two fleshy blobs guarding her valley.

Pradeep sir Do some thing, she wanted to yell but words being cut by teeth.

Pradeep got his hand released and asked Maitreyi,' Its bad, you are my student.'

'Sorry sir,' she was remorse.

Soon she would make him forget student teacher relations, they would have physical union which was started in 12 th standard what was he talking now, and her parents were trying to make him his man, she had to teach a sesson to Vibha also, how could she misbehave with her, marriage or no marriage, she should learn a lesson, she was determined.

Finding her depressed Pradeep realized his folly and said, 'I am sorry Maitreyi, I did not mean that.'

'Sir, my parents would marry me to you. In a fit of sensuality I could do that without realizing that I should not have done that, I am so sorry I have seen girls have so many boy frinds and quench their thirst, they discuss their acts which made me excited. I am so sorry.'

Pradeep was also in remorse what she had done, she was just massaging her by his hand, he should not made her realize that she had

done something wrong, he immdiately took her in his grasp and said,'
Maitreyi you are mine, my woman.'

She rested her head against his chest.

Pradeep lowered his face and straightening her face put his lips over
hers, sudden rush of blood happened in both bodies.

He would caress and fondle what she wanted, **she had understood the
power of feminine sexuality.**

She asked separating, 'Sir should I come to the apartment tonight?'

He looked at her.

'Sir you are my man, you have to teach me plastic surgery.'

'Yes, come, I will teach you anatomy of inguinal hernia in detail.'

'Yes sir.'

Maitreyi went away.

What this girl wanted from him, Sex? He did not know, but she said he
was his man, she might be sure of marriage, and what she said that
girls had lot of boy friends and did many such things of which she
had no opportunity, girls at this age wanted to explore, and she was
exploring how a man's hand caressing her genitals feel like; otherwise
she was a girl and had no boy friends that must be the reason of her
being stimulated to that extent.

Sir you have removed your hand, tonight you would put hand yourself.
I know how to tame the man, I have tamed so many already, I would
tame you also, sir, and take revenge from Vibha who had misbehaved
with me.

Pradeep was at his apartment when Maitreyi called him over phone,
'Sir may I come now, I am so scared of Vibha madam.'

'You may come.'

'Sir, Vibha madam, I am so scared of her.'

'There is no reason to be scared, she wont come today and if she came he would manage. Maitreyi come in nice dress, I mean fully covered.'

'In burqua sir?' she giggled.

'Not in burqua but something like that.'

'Sir, I shall come in salwar suit as a nice girl,' she said and continued to think that he would caress from where he removed his hand.

Maitreyi seems to be good girl, ecstatic like Neelima but having no guests to wander over in her ectstaic dale, it was what she had said that other girls had many boy friends and did lot of filthy things while she did not have one. Those girls might be telling many incidences of sex, which must have been arousing her, and so she could not control herself and clutched his hand to bring that down. But she realized her folly and was in remorse, Pradeep thought. Maitreyi came and knocked at the door, Pradeep opened door and found Maitreyi over there, 'Come Maitreyi,' Pradeep called him inside.

She came and sat over the sofa. Clad in salwar suit she was appearing more sensuous than in skimpy clothes in which she had come yesterday.

'So I will tell you anatomy of inguinal hernia and the canal,' he said and came nearer to her. 'Just stand up,' he requested.

'Sir, please tell me on note book, that would suffice.'

'Yes,' Pradeep took hold of the note book which she had brought out from her bag. 'This is inguinal canal,' Pradeep drew the canal, but he was not feeling good, he had asked her to come to apartment so that he could tell her the actual inguinal canal and not to teach her by diagrams. But Pradeep you was the one who removed the hand when she was taking you to the ecstacy. Now just draw on paper and be satisfied. She was a good girl, it was only due to some thoughts that she must have been stimulated and clutched his hand and took where she wanted to get caressed. But now he had to be satisfied by teaching her on the paper.

'This is superficial inguinal ring, situated just nearby the clitoris, I will tell you where, he pointed her to get up and let him show.'

'Sir I can understand, by your drawing.'

'You wont get the idea.'

'Sir, if Vibha madam comes she would scold at me and you both.'

'No, she wont come.'

'Sir teach me on paper only,' she persisted.

Pradeep sir, **I will make you a doggy with tongue out side and drooling the saliva, I know how to conquer the males.**

She was simple girl, he took her wrong and insulted when she was clutching his hand and getting caresses over her valley, but then he became preacher and removed his hand and insulted her, now he was longing to do what he denied himself.

Pradeep taught her the anatomy of the cananl in detail, when she got up and thanked, 'Thank you sir, you taught me in detail so that I could understand,' she again thanked Pradeep.

'Sir,' she said sensuously, 'I like you.'

And Pradeep was lanced inside. She was going and he could not dare to kiss her, she might refuse, and even her bosom was enshrouded in a way that nothing could be seen. 'Sir I am going,' she said and walked to gate when Pardeep clutched her hand, 'I like you too much Maitreyi.' She turned and peeped directly in his eyes and was to say something when they sighted Vibha and both parted away hurriedly.

'What was happening?' Vibha asked.

'She had come for studies.'

'What studies! I am unable to undertand, why cant you teach her at college, and call her here in the apartment. And why you were holding her hand,' she hollered, 'Pradeep, now it is too much, what has happened to you, you are not the same person who has not bothered for the herds of women swarming you, but now I am seeing that you have become perfect womanizer, and not bother for any relation, she is your student and you are not leaving her also.'

'What I have done?'

'What else you wanted to do, you were holding her hand, might have kissed her and what else you wanted to do,' she squeaked', 'Want to ravish her, to make her pregnant, want to be father of hers; what else you want to do?' she was stern.

'Vibha I have not done any thing like that, come inside,' he said making room for her to enter.

'No I am not coming inside, call Shreya, Maitreyi, Nalini, Neelima, there are so many, for you to call. I think I have no space for me in this apartment,' she turned to go out.

'Vibha,' he clutched her shoulder, but she bent and wriggle out of his clutch and mountained down. 'Vibha,' he again called her, but she did not stop back and went away.

Gone, what was she thinking was perhaps right, he had become womanizer in right sense, he had ravished Neelima, ate the fruits of her beautiful grove, wanted to ravish Maitreyi as well and one day he would eat the fruits of her grove as well; and what was wrong in that. Both were willing for this. Why a student should have come at his apartment, for what. She had come to his apartment but there was no allegation for her, all allegations were for him, he had become womanizer had become immoral. She had gone. But he did not know how to tell that **for a man sensuouslity of female body is as important as other things** and he was sorry to say that Vibha was not able to arouse him sensually, and when he wanted to caress her boobs, she would fritter away. Why to be so moral that not to allow to kiss the boobs.

This man had become mad for women, Vibha was thinking. Neelima had infatuated him and she was tryimg to get rid of her and now Maitreyi had come, from whom she could not get rid off, because she had to stay over here. My god, the only thing could help her was to marry soon, but in these circumastances she was not going to marry him, she would not marry a womanizer. If after marriage he continued to meet Neelima or Maitreyi or somebody else, what would she do, at what place she would be, she would not be able to do any thing. If he wanted to marry her he had to prove that he was not interested in any other woman, and then onward he would stop meeting any of the woman.

Pradeeo opened the chamber when registrar came to take him for the rounds. After the rounds he was waiting for Vibha, but she did not come, instead Maitreyi came.

'Sir, how are you? Vibha madam said something? ?'

Pradeep looked at her and smiled, 'What she would have said. Was not happy with your presence.'

She was envious of me, she thought that all women are alike, she could not be different; no woman could tolerate presence of other woman with her supposed to be man, Vibha madam must be thinking that pradeep sir was his man. But why Pradeep sir would bother for her. No gorgeous body, small boobs, why sir would be at all interested in her.

'Sir I could understand the inguinal canal very well, Please teach me cancer breasts also sometime.'

'No problem.'

'When do you want?'

'Any time and any where sir,' she spelled sensuously.

Pradeep missed many heart beats. 'Sir I love you and for you I can come anywhere. I am not scared of you, ususally I don't move with any boy but you are different sir, different from everybody.'

Pradeep was feeling the pulsations inside his flesh, Maitreyi wanted to give her something, may be her virginity, was she virgin, he thought, must be. if she was so scared of rooming around with boys, she had to be celibate. And she thought him so differntly. Yes he was different.

Sir I will make you my doggy, I know that.

'Then you can come to apartment.'

'Today?'

'Yes.'

'At what time?'

'Same, at 6 pm.'

'Ok sir,' she said and went out side.

When he went to apartment he forgot that Vibha had not come that day, he was lost in Maitreyi and in front of her Vibha stood at no place.

Maitreyi came in the evening. 'How are you she asked?' bewitching smile spread over her lips which baffled Pradeep, he made the way for her to enter inside the apartment and bolting the door from inside came to her.

'So what will you take?'

'Sir, I will prepare tea for you also,' said she and went inside the kitchen, kept the water to boil when Pradeep came, 'Got every thing?'

'Yes,' she answered and then asked, 'Where is sugar?'

'In the upper cabinet.'

She stepped up to one of the cabinet, when she fell and was hurriedly held in his arms by Pradeep to avoid her falling, her boobs were cupped by him. 'Sorry sir,' she did not try to straighten her. 'It's alright,' Pradeep asked not to try to straighten and kept on cupping her boobs. She gave the bewitching smile. 'Sir you are so sweet!'

She brought the tray with cups of tea in drawing hall and gave one cup to him. Pradeep clutched her hand and pushed her to sit beside her.

'Sir,' she said rejoicing sitting buy his side.

After tea, Pradep asked,' So you wanted to learn cancer of the breasts?'

'Yes sir.'

'Cancer of breasts is caused by unknown reasons but is more common in infertile women, for early detection the breasts should be examined every month. I will tell, you how it should be done. Stand up,' he asked her to stand up and move her arm up, she could remove her suit so that she could an understand better. 'Sir explain, I will just understand,' she was not in mood to expose herself. 'Sir I will make you my doggy,' she thought.

After detailing about cancer breasts and self examination, he told there was no problem if she came every evening for studies.

'Sir, when are you going to Delhi?'

'On Saturday.'

'Then come with us and this time stay with us,' she requested.

Pradeep was noncommittal.

Back to hostel she was thinking that she would made him her doggy and he would do what she would tell him to do.

Maitreyi he would stay in her house, he wanted to adorn her garden, water the plants in her garden, he thought. Neelima was bad character girl and he would not marry to her, but Maitreyi was suitable, innocent and fit to be married.

At the same time Neelima called her, 'Pradeep when are you coming, never call me, I am missing you. Are you coming on Friday?'

'No Neelima I can not come on Friday.'

'Why?' she squeaked.

'I have some work.'

'Pradeep I am dying over here, you have to come.'

'Neelima try to understand, my mother is not well, I am going to Agra.'

'Pradeep, I am missing you. Alright, I can't do any thing when your mother is ill. But don't change the programme of Sunday.'

How to get rid off her, Pradeep thought. She was characterless girl, and he could not marry to this girl, but how to get rid off her. If he wanted to get rid off her, he should forget to shift to Delhi, at least for time being.

But he should not refuse Neelima straight, her boobs are really ecstatic, and he developed sudden urge to rush to Delhi and cup her boobs.

Should he go to Delhi on Friday? What about Maitreyi? She wont allow him to touch at her boobs while Neelima would give him the opportunity to play with and feel the warmth of her body.

Pradeep opened the door of chamber when registrar came for the round. He asked registrar to take the round of all the patients and inform him. He went away. Vibha did not come that day also. Would she not come at all, she had to be cajoled. In the evening he would go to her apartment, he thought. Maitreyi came.

'Good morning sir, how are you?' Same bewitching smile which thrilled Pradeep.

'I am fine and how are you?'

'I am also fine, sir what will you teach me today?'

'What you want to be taught?'

'Whatever you want to teach sir.'

Pradeep thought for a while and then told she should come in the evening, he would teach some thing.

'What sir?'

'Something, come in the evening.'

'Ok sir.'

Registrar came and informed that everything was alright in the ward, all patients were doing well.

In the evening Pradeep wanted to go to the apartment of Vibha when Maitreyi came, 'Come Maitreyi,' Pradeep became fluid seeing her.

She sauntered and sat on sofa. 'What do you want to study today?' he asked 'Whatever you wanted to tell sir,' she answered sensuously.

'Ok, give me your palm.'

'Palm! 'she stretched her hand to keep her palm over his hand.

'I will teach you palmistry.'

'Ok.' she giggled.

He stretched her hand and put over his lips.

'Sir you are reading my palm with lips, is this new technique?'

'Yes, devised by Dr Pradeep.'

'Oh!' she said sensuously and giggled.

Suddenly Pradeep got up and took her in embrace.

'Sir which study you are teaching?' she asked giggling.

'Lip to palm reading.'

'Oh!' she giggled again, Pradeep was having rush of the blood all over his body and he lowered his lips over her neck.

'Sir I think this much study is sufficient for today.'

'Is it so?'

'Yes sir, 'she said and giggled which aroused him further and he insinuated his fingers beneath her bra to caress her boobs, when she clutched his hand and said sternly, 'Sir this much study is sufficient for today.'

Pradeep removed his hand and laughed.

He did not go to Vibha's apartment. When Maitreyi went away he thought he should go to her.

He went to Vibha's apartment when maitreyi went away. Vibha opened the gate, 'What happened, Maitreyi has not come to day?'

'She had come but . . .'

'She had come,' she squeaked, 'She had come, even after I told you not to entertain her at apartment. Get lost and never come to me,' She roared and thrusted him out and bolted the door.

What this man think, no shame, saying she had come. Praeeep you are changed man now and not my type of man. Forget Vibha.

What had happeed to you Vibha Pradeep was thinking returning to his apartment.

When he reached the apartment, Neelima called him, 'So are you coming tomorrow?'

'Neelima I am going to Agra and it would not be possible to come to Delhi tomorrow.'

'Pradeep I will die. I miss you so much that I cant live without you.'

'Neelima my mother is not well, so I may come directly to nursing home on Sunday.'

'No way Pradeep you are coming on Friday.'

'Ok I will monitor my mother's condition and then decide,' he said.

Though he wanted to forget Neelima but when she called, he felt immediate urge to caress her boobs and her thighs, caress her flesh of boobs, tiny little flesh which he sucked so many times and she was aroused. No, he was going to Delhi on Friday, he changed his mind. Maitreyi wont allow him to caress her boobs, while Neelima was always there with naked body, so why should he worry for Maitreyi, he would go to Neelima who was waiting for him with open fleshy masses protecting the ecststaic valley of hers.

Pradeep opened the chamber when registrar came for the round. Pradeep asked him to take the round and inform him the condition of the patients, he also informed the registrar that he would be on leave on Friday and Saturday so he should manage the patients and ward accordingly. Registrar agreed and went away.

Vibha had misbehaved with him. It was too insulting when she turned him away, but what else she should have done. How could a woman accept some other woman with his man. Pradeep are you womanizer. He did not know. What ever he was, there was no doubt that from these two women he had developed infatuation. He was determined not to go to Delhi on Friday, but suddenly he develped longing to be with her, to caress her boobs, her thighs and her naked body all over and he could not conrol him self deciding to go to her on Friday. Maitreyi, he was not able to understand, she must be a good girl unadorned celibate, might be good for marriage, while Neelima was not good for marriage. Vibha, I could not undertsand, she behaved very badly yesterday.

Vibha developed an urge to go to Pradeep, she should not have insulted Pradeep and turned him away. He was her man. No doubt he was enticed by two women, **but women body could entice any man, it is true every where and in every part of the world.** She should protect Pradeep from these two witches rather than insult him.

She got up and was in dilemma whether to go to Prdaeep or not, she walked oblivious of the fact that she turned to the chamber of pradeep. 'Vibha,' Pradeep greeted by standing and getting to his feet, 'I am missing you.'

Vibha came in his embrace, 'Pradeep I am sorry for my behaviour which I should not have done.' Pradeep lowered his face and kissed her, 'Vibha you are my woman, you have turned me out, but I did not feel bad, a normal woman should have done so. How could a woman accept her man seducing the other woman.'

Vibha looked at Pradeep through the haze of saline water in front of her eyes and could see Pradeep in parts. Oh pradeep she let herself go loose in his arms and saline water flowed from four eyes.

He would not go to Neelima next day he thought when Vibha went away, he should control himself, or else he would lose Vibha, she was the woman suitable for marriage.

Maitreyi came to his chamber, 'How are you sir?'

'I am fine Maitreyi and how are you?'

She came nearer to his table and stooped so that her boobs were visible, naked flesh of her boobs . . . glimpses of her naked flesh of boobs aroused him and he felt rush of blood all over his body.

'Sir, yesterday you told me palmistry and lip-palmistry,' she commented sensuously, 'What about today?'

'Today, I will teach you about ecstatic valley.'

'What is that?' Maitreyi understood what he said, but posed as if she could not understand what he said.'

'Valley!What valley sir?'

'Come in evening I will teach you different valleys and how to visit them.'

'Ok, sir,' she giggled.

When Maitreyi went away he thought if vibha came the same time as Maitreyi, then every thing would go haywire. He planned that if Vibha came he would ask Maitreyi not to come at apartment. Maitreyi was clever girl, she would understand. On first day when vibha came she immediately put on the apron to hide her body from her gaze, she was naked for Pradeep only and not for others to have glimpses.

In the evening Maitreyi came in salwar suite. 'Pradeep sir, I understand every thing, I will just make you my doggy.' Pradeep opened the door.

He grinned. 'today I will teach you valleys and how to enter in the other valleys.'

She giggled, 'Teach me sir.'

'You mean sir dalliance acts and how to perform?'

He grinned.

'You want to know that.'

'But sir, when you are about to enter then you should know. I mean when you are going to be married. I do not believe in sex before marriage, so this knowedge would not be of use to me, any way sir my parents are bent upon my marriage to you, so you can teach me after marriage, practically,' she giggled. After sometime she went away.

Fortunately vibha did not come when she was there in his apartment. So he went to her apartment after Maitreyi had gone. Vibha welcomed him, 'No Maitreyi today?' She asked.

'Vibha, it is enough.'

'Sorry.'

'Tomorrow I am going to delhi . . . err I mean Agra,' he slurred.

'When will you return?'

'Sunday evening.'

She came in his arms, 'Pradeep I miss you a lot, let us marry.'

'Yes, Vibha, I would talk to my parents also, it would be ok,' Pradeep consoled her. Vibha was content with Pradeep. He was her man, even if he kissed her, it did not matter, **God has created males and all males in that way;** but he was my man, that's all.

Back in apartment, there was call from Neelima. 'Pradeep are you coming tomorrow?'

'Yes.'

'I will pick you up at station.'

'And what will you do?'

'I will take you in car and make you naked, hold your tough organ and take that to valley of fruits,' she giggled.

Pradeep laughed, 'So you would do everything at station itself.'

'Not at station but in car, it can be done in car.'

Pardeep was aroused and developed sudden urge to run and be in arms of Neelima kissing her boobs, her boobs always made him mad with passion and she let her self go in his arms and let him go inside her body. While other women, they always talk of marriage; he could not understand their psyche. What is marriage. Why sex cant be there without marriage. Maitreyi, she was not interested in talking about different postures, Vibha she was not interested in letting him kiss at her boobs.

Maitrey was going to the hostel and thought she understood everything, but she wont allow him to see her naked body before marriage otherwise charm of exploring each other's body vanished away. He must be thinking that she was moron celibate, and she giggled.

Next day Pradeep went to Delhi. In the train he was lost in Neelima, her bare body radiating feminine aura and her ecstatic valley overflowing with liquids. Neelima was at station when he got down. Clad in tight blue jeans and black short top over her bosom, she was superb. She shook his hand and caressed for longer than required to shake the hand, Pradeep smiled. 'Every thing in car.'

She giggled. Holding one of his case they went to the the car parked out side the station. She unlocked the car and sat on driver's seat, Pradeep entering from other side. 'So every thing in car?'

'Yes,' she giggled.

Pradeep got the glimpses of her evections, suddenly turned and lowering his face put his lips over her naked flesh at upper part of shirt.

'Ah!Pradeep what are you doing,' she clutched his hand, unbuttoned her jeans and put his hand over the beautifully arranged tuft of hair.

'Pradeep I miss you so much, now you wont go back to Aligarh.'

Pradeep was caressing her hair which was arousing her too much and in a frenzied attack she took his lips inside her mouth as if to suck the whole nectar of masculine youth.

'Ah Neelima!' He was reclining on seat with half opened eyes, becoming fluid, and feeling happy of Neelima sucking the fluid, of his masculinity, which was pumping more blood to his organ to make that turgid, he being wildly aroused, but trying to control himself he requested, 'We should not complete every thing in car, Neelima?'

'Let it be done.'

'Let us go home, we would do there,' Pradeep reasoned.

'We would do there again, let it be done.'

'Neelima, people may see us, it will be so embarrassing.'

'Pradeep don't . . . don't bring people in our way,' then she straightend up'Ok at home ', she said and giggled. The giggle which was enough to arouse the sensuous feelings, the giggle which caused intensified flow of the blood to the masculine flesh giggle which made him fluid and that flew over her naked flesh . . .

Racing the car she reached the home where she parked the car and got down, Pradeep got down from other side, 'We would be together in room the whole day.'

'Oh, you would kill me.'

'I will rape you, ravish you till my last drop of fuid waters your garden, not even a drop is left behind to water any other woman.'

Neelima giggled, 'Is it so, **but I am sure you would run away without your fluid being wetting my field.'**

'No, it wont happen, rather you will cry of excessive wetness which will take months to dry up again.

Neelima giggled, 'You want to water other women also, your assistant? She is not worth watering, you should water the beautiful orchard so that they blossom.

Pradeep and Neelima came inside house, he went upstairs in the room he had stayed before. Neelima came in the room after some time, 'I have aksed the maid to serve the breakfast over here,' she said and came in his embrace, 'Pradeep I miss you too much, this time you wont go anywhere, and forget your assistant or that student of yours; rememeber only one woman in your family and she is Neelima, explore only one woman and she is Neelima, water only one woman and she is Neelima.'

Pradeep looked at her and grinned.

'And Neelima you should also let one man feel the sensuality of naked flesh of your valley.'

She laughed. 'You are right, you are my man, why should I go to other.'

As there was nothing to do after breakfast he lay on bed joined by Neelima by his side.

They slept for two hours, pleasurable sleep it was, at about 12 Pradeep opened his eyes to find Neelima by his side, her magnificent protrusions out of her shirt, he opened the buttons of shirt and both of her protrusions were naked in front of him, he lowered his face kept the lips over the protrusions and slowly took the fleshy knob in her mouth to try to take out her juice, when she opened her eyes.

'Oh!what are you doing!!' her eyes were wide in surprise.

Pradeep did not answer and kept on sucking, 'Hey man, what areyou doing, taking the advantage of my position.'

Pradeep grinned but did not remover his mouth from over her tiny flesh which had become hard by then.

'Man what are you doing?' She spelled again but sure not to get an answer.

Pradeep did not budge and started sucking more fiercely.

'Ah Pradeep! What are you doing!! I am on the peak of ecstacy,' she said clutching his hand and put over her abdomen. He caressed her abdomen and let himself go loose, his hand was caressing abdomen and decending down to the bush, the bush of nice hair, bush of ecstacy, bush of feminity and bush of arousal, Neelima could not remain loose for long, her body tensed when his hand lowerd to her small fleshy knob and she suddenly slid her hand for his manly flesh which was throbbibg and pulsating; she softly removed the outer protective peel from over the head of the flesh, to take Pradeep at the peak of ecstacy, Neelima also writhed, and moved the peel of skin over the head of his flesh, for many a times, which tensed his body and he jumped to come over her, pulled her thighs wide apart to bring his tongue over the fleshy masses guarding the garden of her ecstaic valley, touch of tongue with flesh ignited her and she clutched his flesh, his hard flesh firmly and put over the entrance, Pradeep go for a run, not stroll, run, fast and fast, and he inserted the flesh with a thug, and ran, ran from one corner to other searching for pleasure in her valley, both interwined, and when they found every bit of pleasure he watered her garden, which gave them what they were searching for, an pleasurable orgasm, ecstatic orgam and they both became loose to take another round of sleep with their naked bodies lying side by side, the warmth of their bodies insinuating in each other.

Pradeep had to go to Agra and he would talk to his parents as she wanted the marriage to take place sooner, her man was being enticed by two powerful women, sexy women; and it was becomimg difficult to protect her man, Vibha thought in her chamber when her man was watering the body of Neelima to quench her thirst and in the process get relieved of overflowing water in his body.

Pradeep woke up again at 2 pm, Neelima was already woken up and was waiting for him to be awake. 'I am going for a discussion, maid would serve lunch, I would return back after few hours, She put her lips over his and gave a powerful kiss.

Pradeep took the lunch and again went to sleep, it was deep sleep of mirth, of dehydration as all of his water was drained out while she was giggling, looking at her body radiating the warmth specially after getting water which she needed immediately.

His sleep was disturbed when some sounds were emanating from the adjacent room. Who? She or he could be?'

Neelima with some other person, he thought.

He developed curiosity and taking the stool to the bathroom mountained up to peep into the other room. and he was aghast, life less, limp and fell down . . .

His body was drenched in sweat, sweat of humiliation, sweat of rising anger, and sweat of contempt . . .

Neelima I will kill you, from now you are not my woman, too mean, witch, as Vibha used to call. And this is the end of our relations, no way, even he can not dare to come again in that house after that scene in which she was lying on her back, legs apart and the man was positioned to water her. That was the end of story, Neelima tomorrow mornig he was going back to Aligarh and On Sunday come again with Maitreyi. Enough is done. How could he tolerate her with some other man in compromising position.

Pulling his legs, came in the room and lay on bed panting for breath, at the same time **Neelima was also panting for breath, panting for breath of ecstcy, of pleasure, or orgasm and Padeep was panting for breath of disillusionment, insult and infidelity . . .**

Vibha called him to enquire the condition of his mother, 'How is your mother?'

'Mother is fine and I am coming back tomorrow.'

'So nice, and have you talked about our marraiage?'

'Yes, I have talked about our marriage on positive note, I will discuss with you tomorrow.'

'I am missing you, come soon,' she said.

Vibha was the right woman for him, he was drifted for time being but this scene of today had released him off Neelima as a bad debt and now Vibha had to be his woman . . .

And what about Maitreyi, she was more gorgeous than Neelima and at the same time disciplined girl, while Neelima was wandering for lust everywhere. She chose me and was clinging to me only, he thought while Neelima . . . No talk of Neelima she was written off.

In the night Neelima came in his room, 'Oh still asleep,' she giggled. Pradeep looked at her . . . giggling of not human being, how a bitch was giggling . . . 'I am feeling too tired, 'Padeep told,' I have just got a a call from home in Agra that mother was not alright and I have to go to Agra in the morning.

'No way Pradeep.'

'Neelima try to understand, he persuaded Neelima.'

Pradeep returned to Aligarh and went to hospital. One of the chapter was closed. Neelima was no more in picture.

Vibha came. 'How is mother?'

'She is alright and in good health.'

'What about marriage?'

'I will talk sometime later if you don't mind,' Pradeep told.

'Ok.'

After Vibha went away Maitreyi came.

'How are you sir, I missed you a lot in the evening.'

'Come today evening.'

'And sir you are coming with us to Delhi.'

'Yes,' he agreed.

In the evening he called Maitreyi and asked her to come early so that by the time she left, Vibha would not have come.

'Sir forget Vibha,' she said and giggled.

She came in half an hour, 'Sir what you will teach today?' she giggled.

'What you wish to be taught?'

'Same palm to lip reading.'

'Oh you want to be expert of palm to lip reading.'

'Yes, sir.'

Pradeep clutched her hand and tried to search the sensuality by his index finger, so soft and so sensuous.

And suddenly he lifted her hand to put over his lips, mere touch of her hand over his lips was sensuous, ecstatic that he could not help him from being aroused and pulled her in her lap, her boobs touching his mighty chest . . .

Maitreyi let herself go loose in his arms.

'Sir . . . I love you.'

Putting his hand down he put his hand over her prodding protuebrances when she stopped him, 'Sir lecture is palm to lip reading and you are trying to teach palm to boob reading, it not nice, limit your self to palm to lip reading only sir,' she said and giggled.

When Maitreyi went away, there was a call from Neelima. 'Pradeep I am missing you a lot, when are you coming back to Delhi?'

'Neelima I cant assure anything, may be I am not able to come to Delhi in near future, as I have to be with my mother for quite sometime.'

'Don't spell like that Pradeep, I am dying to see you to feel you, to feel your pulstaions of rocky hard organ, ready to tear me, my trees of garden into pieces . . .'

'Neelima I cant help.'

'Don't say like that, if you wont come, I would come to Aligarh.'

Pradeep was bewildered, it would not be easy to get rid off her, what to do, he was not able to decide, scratched his head, what to do.

Next day Pradeep went with Maitreyi to Delhi, she and her parents welcomed him warmly. Maitreyi is to be his women, Pradeep thought, sensuous like Neelima and celibate like Vibha, unadorned, celibate and at the same time sensuous, what else he wanted in a wife; she would be his woman.

Pradeep stayed in the room, where miatreyi came in the evening, 'Will you like to go for movie or visit some place? We don't want to bore you.'

Pradeep took her in his arms, 'You are with me, why should I be bored!'

'Hey sir, my parents would see and object,' she said and drifted away.

They are orthodox, planning to marry her to me, already talked to his mother over the phone, Pradeep thought.

'I am yours sir, she took his hand and put over her bosom inside her bra,' it is for you, 'just for time being, till we are married, we have to control.'

Pradeep moved his hand over her sensuous skin of breasts and searched for the small flesh, tender flesh, flesh of sensuality and when he touched, she cried in pleasure, 'Sir, somebody would see.' Without caring for her, he hurriedly tore her bra and her blooosmimg youth was in front of him, he immediately put the flesh in his mouth and sucked that. Maitreyi was unable to do something, she was in fact was not interested to do, she was ignited and wanted him to quench her thirst:with great efforts she separated, 'Sir after marriage, Please don't mind, I do need you inside me as you are aroused so am I, but sir . . . this act after marriage.'

If I give you what you want, you wont marry me sir, it is usual with every man and every male is alike; I am burning inside. She rested her head against his chest ', Sir I am wet, ignited, what to do, do something but not sex . . .'

Pradeep retuned with Maitreyi the next day and went straight to the hospital, he had made up his mind that he would marry Maitreyi.

In the evening Maitreyi did not come, instead when in the night Pradeep was returning from the market somebody could be spotted in the park who they could be.

He called who was there. One shadow ran away an other could not run to whom Pradeep clutched and turned to see her face.

Pradeep went to the apartment of Vibha in the night and told Vibha that his parents were not agreed for the marriage because she was from lower caste, so he had decided to go for court marriage next day.

'Tomorrow! so soon,' Vibha galloped.

'Why? Are you scared?'

'Not scared,' she came in his arms, but she was non committal and said, 'Alright if you decided so, let us go for court marriage. We will go for court marraige and next day we would go to lonavala for honeymoon.'

'Ah!Every thing well planned.'

They married and went to honeymoon. Sitting on the verandah they were looking at mountains and the scenic beauty, Pradeep took her in arms and kissed her; She let herself loose in his arms when he insinuated his fingers beneath her bra and she did not prevent him this time, she was his woman now.

He pulled her inside the room and caressed her bosom, abdomen and flesh which was throbbing for the first time, he was aroused and raced for sexual act to take her at the peak of ecstacy . . . orgasm after orgasm with her own man, she was bruised, bruising of pleasurable sexual act, bruising by her man and she enjoyed the pleasurable pain from the bruisings.

He suddenly decided to marry because Neelima was ruled out and Maitreyi was also ruled out . . . Maitreyi was ruled out when he caught her in the park, he was shattered, shattered in the pieces; every organ of his was torn and broken, bruised and swollen . . . And suddenly he decided to go to Vibha . . .

They returned after 5 days and Vibha shifted her apartment to Pradeep's, but at the same time Neelima came, where were you Pradeep your phone was switched off . . .

'We had gone for honeymoon,' Vibha teased her.

'Honeymoon? With whom? How can it be possible?'

'Why?'

'He is my man.'

'Now he is my man.'

'Madam he cant marry you.'

'Why?'

'Becase he had promised to marry me and had sex with me.'

'All are the things of past, fact is that he is my man, my husband, legal one.'

'He can not do it, I will put him behind the bar.'

'How?'

'He had sex with me,' Pradeep tell her this is all true, you are my man, you had sex with me, you loved me, you are my man . . .'

Pradeep did not say a word.

'Ok if you dont speak a word, I would be free to do what I liked.'

'What?' Vibha screamed.

'I will prove he had sex with me.'

'How?'

'Vibha, it is Neelima. I have his semen on my panty and that is preserved, DNA testing would prove that he had sex with me and he would be behind the bar for 7years. He is my man so I wont like to do so against him, but if there is no option, I will do it.'

'What do you want Neelima?' Pradeep asked.

'Come to me,' she grabbed him, 'Come Neelima is yours.'

'But now I am married.'

'Does not matter, come to me and she started kissing him fiercely, wetting his face with saline water, I cant live without you Pradeep.'

And the love triangle continues . . . .

About the Author

Dr Vishwa Prakash is plastic surgeon by profession and writing is his hobby. He writes English and Hindi novels and poems. He has written about one hundred Hindi stories. Dr Vishwa Prakash is well known novelist whose three novels are already published—The last Chapter, The Virgin Beauty and Kamali—The Courage. It is his fourth novel.

And
Love
Triangle
Continues